Hope Valley High

IZZY's UNEXpECTED WEEK

Emily Owen

Authentic

First published 2024 by Authentic Media Limited,
PO Box 6326, Bletchley, Milton Keynes, MK1 9GG.
authenticmedia.co.uk

British Library Cataloguing in Publication Data
A catalogue record for this book is available from the British Library.
ISBN: 978-1-78893-314-8
978-1-78893-315-5 (e-book)

Cover design and illustrations by Beatriz Albano

Printed and bound by CPI Group (UK) Ltd, Croydon, CR0 4YY

My name: Izzy

My age: 11

My hair colour: Brown

My eye colour: Blue

I live with: Mum and Dad

My favourite place: Gran's house

My school: Hope Valley High School for Girls

I am in year: 7

Fact about me: I like pizza

My best friend: Jo

My favourite joke: What is the easiest animal to weigh?
A fish, because it has its own scales!

Izzy slammed the front door behind her. Dropping her bag at the bottom of the stairs, she kicked off her shoes and headed for the kitchen.

What a RUBBISH day.

It had started with a maths test. Izzy didn't like maths, and the test had put her in a bad mood. She knew she hadn't done well. Then at break time, she'd been walking to meet her friends and had tripped over, right in the middle of the corridor. A group of Year 9s saw her. Izzy was so embarrassed. Year 9s didn't like Year 7s, and she had planned to sneak past them. Instead, she fell flat on her face. Great.

Then, when she got to her friends out on the playing field and told them what happened, Jo laughed. What a traitor.

Izzy looked in the fridge. None of her favourite snacks left in there. The day was just getting better and better.

Slamming the fridge door shut, like she'd slammed the front door, Izzy grabbed an apple from the fruit bowl. She was halfway up the stairs when she heard Mum calling her.

What now? Izzy turned, stomped down the stairs, and put her head round the door of the sitting room. 'What?'

'Come in here a minute. I need to tell you something…'

With a sigh that was more like a **HUFF**, Izzy went and sat down, taking a bite from her apple as Mum began to talk.

The more Mum talked, the more Izzy couldn't believe what she was hearing. The apple slipped from her hand, and she stared at Mum.

'I'm not staying with *HER!* Can't I come with you to see Gran?'

Izzy loved her Gran. Gran was the best. She lived at the seaside in a little house that was full of things to look at. She had a teddy bear whose fur had nearly all fallen off, but Gran wouldn't get rid of him. 'He's grown up with me, Izzy, and now he's old like me,' she'd say. 'I can't get rid of him just because he's old.' Teddy had 'Izzy' sewn in red on the bottom of his left foot.

Whenever Izzy went to stay at Gran's house, Teddy was always there on her bed. At home, nearly all her toys were up in the attic now, but she liked having Teddy at Gran's. He'd been there her whole life. Sometimes she even talked to him. Was she too big to do that now she was 11, and in Year 7? If anyone at school knew she talked to Teddy, they'd laugh at her and never let her forget it. Especially Suzy. Suzy was mean to everyone.

Izzy's bedroom at Gran's was up a little staircase, and had a ceiling that sloped two ways. Izzy had to be careful not to bump her head! There was a little window and, if she knelt on her bed and opened the window, she could smell the sea. Sea-smell was one of Izzy's favourite smells.

It was great at Gran's house.

Sometimes, Gran baked cakes, and Izzy helped. Gran had a special apron for Izzy, which was kept on the peg beside Gran's own apron. When they made cakes, the first thing they did was put their aprons on. Gran's apron said 'I like hugs' on it, so Izzy always gave her a big hug. Izzy's arms round Gran's waist, Gran's arms around Izzy, Izzy didn't know who was hugging who! She stayed there for as long as she could. She felt **safe**.

Izzy's apron had a big red heart on it, with her name inside. 'Izzy'. Gran sewed it on for her, the same as she had sewn on Teddy.

Mum coughed, snapping Izzy out of her daydream and back into the sitting room. She looked at Mum. Izzy really, really, really wanted to go to Gran's. She wanted to go anywhere as long as it wasn't Aunty Elizabeth's. Izzy would rather live in an igloo at the north pole, surrounded by ice and bears, than go to *HER* house.

'Please? Please let me come to Gran's? Please please please please please?'

Mum closed her eyes. Izzy sat up straighter, hoping.

What Izzy didn't know was that sending Izzy to her sister's house was the last thing Mum wanted to do. She'd tried all other options, and no one had been able to help. Calling her sister had been one of the **hardest** things she'd ever done. She could still remember the conversation:

'Will you have your niece to stay while I look after Mum?'

Silence.

'I said, will you . . .'

'Yes, I heard you. Why are you asking me?'

'Because there's no one else.'

'Huh. At least you're honest.'

'And you never do anything for Mum. I don't see you rushing to look after her. When was the last time you even called, let alone saw her?'

'OK, OK, don't start this again. I'll do it.'

End of conversation.

Mum opened her eyes. 'I'm sorry, Izzy, but it's best that you go and stay with your aunt. Dad and I don't want you to miss school, and Gran really needs a holiday.'

Izzy slumped back in her chair. There was no point arguing.

Jumping up, and taking the stairs two at a time, Izzy went to her bedroom and lay down on her bed. She hugged her purple cushion – the one Jo had given her – and wished Teddy was here.

Aunty Elizabeth was Mum's sister, but no one ever talked about her. Ever. All Izzy knew was that a long time ago, Mum and Aunty Elizabeth had a big ARGUMENT and stopped speaking to each other.

Why would I want to stay with someone who won't speak to my mum? Izzy hugged the cushion tighter. *Maybe Aunty Elizabeth won't speak to me either. I look like Mum. And what if she laughs at me, like Jo did? I know Jo didn't laugh in a mean way really, but what if Aunty Elizabeth has a mean laugh?*

She closed her eyes. If only the cushion was a magic one that would make everything alright.

Things must be serious if Mum had asked Aunty Elizabeth if Izzy could stay with her. Mum said Gran needed a holiday, but maybe she was poorly or something.

Izzy could really do with someone to talk to. Even Teddy.

Rolling off the bed, she began to pack. How was she supposed to know what she should take to visit this aunty she didn't know?

She packed clothes and school stuff, making sure not to forget her Word Book. Mrs James had given everyone in the class a Word Book in English lesson that morning. Word Book was a book full of blank pages, and at the end of each day, they had to write in it – something about the day, but they were only allowed up to three words. What a stupid idea. Izzy threw the book into her bag.

Then she took it out, and opened it at the first page. Today didn't need three words, one would do: Rubbish.

Izzy wrote 'Rubbish' in the middle of the page, and underlined the word three times with black pen. Then she drew an angry face next to it. Maybe the face would count as a word.

Saturday

The next day, Mum drove Izzy to Aunty Elizabeth's house. It wasn't far away, so Izzy could still walk to school next week. Izzy looked out of the car window, watching cars and trees and people go by, and wondered if Aunty Elizabeth would bake cakes. Probably not.

When the car was nearly there, Mum pulled over to the side of the road. Izzy felt a **bubble** of hope rising inside her. 'Are we going back? Can I come to Gran's?'

Mum shook her head, 'No. But I do have a surprise for you.'

Not another surprise. Izzy turned away and stared out of the car window. She'd had enough surprises to last a lifetime.

Mum tapped her shoulder, but Izzy didn't turn round. Why should she? She wiped at the tears that pricked her eyes. It wasn't fair. Mum kept tapping until Izzy couldn't ignore it anymore. She turned round. It wasn't Mum tapping her – it was Teddy!

Mum held Teddy out:

'Gran asked me if you'd look after Teddy while we are away. Will you do that?'

Izzy grabbed Teddy and hugged him to her. He smelled like Gran's house.

'OK.' Her voice sounded **wobbly** and strange.

Mum started the car again, and as they drove on, Izzy whispered to Teddy, 'We'll be OK, won't we?'

The car stopped in front of a place that looked just like pictures Izzy had seen in magazines while she waited to see the dentist. She stared. Was it real, or not? Did people really live in places like that?

Climbing out of the car, Mum picked up Izzy's case, and Izzy saw her take a deep breath before firmly walking up to the front door. Izzy trailed after her. Izzy really wanted to run away, but her legs seemed to have a mind of their own. She watched as Mum reached for the doorbell. Mum had red nail varnish on. It was called 'Traffic Light Red'; Izzy knew that because she'd seen the bottle in the bathroom. If only it was a real Traffic Light. Red meant 'stop'. Maybe they could stop this nightmare, and Izzy would wake up and find it had all been a bad dream. Mum pressed the doorbell, then took a step back. Both her hands, with the traffic-light nails, held the case handle tightly. Her knuckles turned white. Mum looked nervous, and Izzy nearly asked if she'd like to hug Teddy. Hugging Teddy always made Izzy feel a bit better. Before she could suggest it, the front door opened. Izzy stared. Aunty Elizabeth was like Mum, but different.

Mum had short hair, Aunty Elizabeth's was longer, but it was the same colour. Mum wore glasses, Aunty Elizabeth didn't, but they both had the same colour eyes. Izzy liked Mum's eyes, they were the colour of the sea she saw from the window at Gran's. She wished she was in her room at Gran's now, kneeling on her bed and looking at the sea.

No one was speaking. Both grown-ups were looking over each other's shoulders. They couldn't even look at each other. Izzy felt tears springing to her eyes again. She didn't normally cry, but she didn't normally have to deal with what was happening at the moment. Blinking hard, she hugged Teddy. Izzy didn't want to stay here in this magazine building, with a woman who didn't speak and wouldn't even look at her. She wanted to stay with Mum. Izzy **sniffed** and Mum looked down at her, as though suddenly remembering she was there.

'Thank you for having Izzy to stay.' Mum looked at Aunty Elizabeth now. She spoke in the polite voice she used with strangers. Mum handed Izzy's case to Aunty Elizabeth, who took it but didn't seem to know what to do with it. Aunty Elizabeth's nails were painted pink. Pink wasn't on traffic lights at all.

Mum bent towards Izzy. 'Be good,' she said. Izzy flung her arms around Mum's neck. She breathed deeply and smelled Mum's perfume. Time to be **BRAVE**. 'I love you,' she whispered into Mum's ear. 'I love you,' Mum whispered back. It was a conversation they always whispered to each other. Eventually, Mum unwrapped Izzy's arms. The tears Izzy had blinked back were on her cheeks now, and Mum gently brushed them away with her thumb. Squeezing Izzy's hand, Mum straightened up. Aunty Elizabeth was still holding the case. Izzy wanted to snatch it back and run to the car. Instead, she took a deep breath, hugged Teddy and waved her mum goodbye.

Izzy looked at Aunty Elizabeth. Aunty Elizabeth looked at Izzy. *Finally, she looked at me*, thought Izzy.

Izzy felt awkward, having Aunty Elizabeth stare at her like that. It didn't occur to her that Aunty Elizabeth might not like being stared at, either.

'You'd better come in,' said Aunty Elizabeth, and Izzy followed her inside.

As soon as they were through the front door, they took their shoes off, and Aunty Elizabeth said she'd show Izzy around.

They walked around the flat, Aunty Elizabeth pointing out different rooms. All Izzy could think about was white. Everything was white! White carpet, white walls, white chairs. She was glad she had taken her shoes off at the front door.

She followed her aunt, nodding.

'That's the sitting room.' Nod. 'That's the bathroom.' Nod.

The last door in the hallway was the room where Izzy would be sleeping. It was quite small, and had a window that reached from the ceiling to the floor. Izzy's eyes were drawn to the window straight away. She had a window, like she did at Gran's! Izzy knew she wouldn't be able to see the sea here, but maybe she'd be able to see trees. Izzy liked trees.

Aunty Elizabeth put the suitcase on the bed.

She looked at Izzy, who was standing **uncertainly** in the doorway. 'Why don't you unpack, and then we'll have a cup of coffee?'

With that, Aunty Elizabeth was gone. Izzy didn't have a chance to tell her that she didn't drink coffee.

Slowly, Izzy walked to the bed and sat down beside her case. She looked around the room. She didn't want to be here. It wasn't like Gran's house, where there was a lot to look at. Here, there was nothing but white.

Through the window, Izzy could see rooves, and buildings, and roads, and cars. She should have known there wouldn't be trees.

She wished she was with Mum and Dad and Gran, not here on her own. She hugged Teddy, who didn't seem to mind when her tears made his head wet, and whispered, 'I wish I was with Gran.' It felt good to tell someone, even Teddy.

Gran had sent Teddy in some new clothes. Izzy wiped her eyes and looked at the clothes properly for the first time. There was a red T-shirt with a tractor picture on the front, and blue jeans. The jeans had a pocket with a zip on. Izzy undid the zip. It was a bit stiff, and she had to jerk it open. There was something inside! Lots of tiny little envelopes! She took them out and they fitted onto her hand. The top envelope had 'Izzy' written on it, in Gran's handwriting. Izzy knew it was Gran's, because it looked the same as the writing in Gran's book, which they used to make cakes. Gran always opened the book at the recipe, but Izzy noticed she never looked at it. The recipe was in Gran's head. How many cakes had Gran made in her life? It must be millions.

Izzy was about to open the top envelope, when she heard Aunty Elizabeth calling her. Oh yes, coffee! Aunty Elizabeth would be waiting for her. Aunty Elizabeth probably didn't like waiting. Izzy was still worried about how to tell her aunt that she didn't like coffee, but she felt a bit better now, because of the envelopes. Putting them back in Teddy's pocket, she carefully closed the zip, left Teddy on the bed and went to the kitchen. In the hallway, she hesitated. Which door was it that led to the kitchen? *The white one*. Izzy rolled her eyes. They were all white. She opened one, but it led to Aunty Elizabeth's office, and Izzy closed the door again quickly. She could hear her heart THUMPING. The next door she tried led to the kitchen.

Aunty Elizabeth was there and, seeing Izzy, asked, 'Do you like milk in your coffee?'

Izzy stood in the doorway, wondering what to say.

'I don't know.'

'You don't know? You don't know how you take your coffee?'

Izzy looked at the floor. 'I don't drink coffee.'

Aunty Elizabeth's eyebrows went up. You'd have thought Izzy had said she'd got three feet or something.

Izzy felt silly for not drinking coffee.

Aunty Elizabeth's eyebrows moved into a slight frown. 'What would you like to drink, then?'

'Can I have some juice?'

There was no juice, so Izzy had a glass of water.

'Later on, we'll go shopping,' said Aunty Elizabeth. 'I don't know what you like to eat and drink, so you'll need to tell me.'

Izzy nodded. She was thinking about her friend Amy. Amy's aunty sometimes met Amy after school. Izzy was sure Amy's aunty knew what to give her to eat and drink.

Izzy and Aunty Elizabeth sat with a table between them. The table felt **longer** than the Eiffel Tower in Paris is tall. More than 300 metres; Izzy had learned that in her French lesson last week.

She fought back tears. It would have been so much better if she could have gone to Gran's with Mum. Thinking about Gran reminded Izzy about Teddy, and the secret envelopes. How soon could she go back to her room? She wanted to get up and walk out of the kitchen, but she didn't dare.

Aunty Elizabeth drank her coffee, and Izzy drank her water, in silence. Then Aunty Elizabeth cleared her throat and said to get ready for shopping. Izzy stood up straight away, so quickly she nearly knocked her chair over. She managed to catch it before it fell on the floor, and pretended she hadn't seen Aunty Elizabeth's frown.

All Izzy needed to do to get ready was put her coat and shoes on, and they were by the front door, but she went to her bedroom. If she was quick, there would be time to open the envelope.

Sitting on the bed, Izzy undid the zip on Teddy's pocket. It was a bit less stiff this time, and she took out the 'Izzy' envelope. Carefully, she opened it. It was very small, and she didn't want it to rip. She pulled out a piece of paper, folded again and again to make it small enough to fit. Izzy unfolded it and laid it on the bed. She smoothed it out, but it still looked as though it was covered in little squares, from the folds. It was a letter from Gran!

Dear Izzy,

I'm sorry you have to stay with Aunty Elizabeth because I've been poorly. I'm getting better now, I hope, but the doctor said a holiday would do me good. Thank you for letting your mum and dad come and take me away for a bit. I know you don't know Aunty Elizabeth, but hopefully you will get to know her.

So Gran *was* poorly. And that's why she needed a holiday. What was the matter with her?

I'm glad you found the letters in Teddy! Don't open them all at once! Take your time with them. They are about a very special new friend of mine.

Love from Gran

Izzy carefully folded the letter, put it back in its envelope, and slipped it into Teddy's pocket with the others.

Maybe things weren't so bad. She had Teddy, she had Gran, and she had letters about Gran's friend. She didn't know Gran had a new friend!

There was still Aunty Elizabeth to deal with, but Izzy felt a bit better.

Aunty Elizabeth! Izzy had forgotten. She put Teddy down on the bed. Time to shop.

Pizza

They went in the car to the supermarket, and Izzy sat in the front passenger seat; there were no back seats. Izzy had never seen a car with just two seats in before! The car was blue but, inside, everything was white. Again. White must be Aunty Elizabeth's favourite colour, thought Izzy, and she wondered if she should take her shoes off. Aunty Elizabeth kept her own shoes on and so Izzy did the same. She sat very still, though, worried that if she moved, she might make the car dirty.

The car was kept in a carpark underneath the flat. The carpark was dark, and when they drove out, Izzy blinked in the sunlight. Aunty Elizabeth put sunglasses on, then pressed a button, and the roof of the car disappeared! Suddenly, Izzy's long brown hair was **blowing** all around her as the car made a wind. It was noisy, too, but that was good, because it meant they couldn't talk. *Not that we'd have talked anyway.* Izzy wrinkled her nose as she remembered the silent coffee and water. It would be a long week if they didn't talk to each other.

Izzy recognized the supermarket. It was the same one she came to with Mum when they did their shopping on Saturdays. Today was Saturday, but Izzy was here with Aunty Elizabeth, not with Mum.

Did Aunty Elizabeth come here every Saturday, too, and if she did, how had they never seen each other? They would have been in the same building!

Aunty Elizabeth parked the car and pressed a button to make the roof go back over their heads. It made Izzy feel as though the world was closing in on her, and she quickly opened the car door and climbed out. She shifted her weight from foot to foot as she waited for her aunty to take off her sunglasses, find her bag and lock the car.

They walked to the supermarket in silence. It felt strange, as though they were together but not together. Izzy had never felt like that with anyone before.

When they reached the trolley park, Aunty Elizabeth pulled at a trolley, but it was stuck inside another. Izzy took hold of the handle and pulled as well. They both needed to pull as hard as they could to get it out, and when it suddenly came out of the other trolley, it nearly made Izzy fall over! She giggled, then stopped, but she thought she saw Aunty Elizabeth SMILING too.

Inside the supermarket, Aunty Elizabeth told Izzy to point out anything she'd like. 'I know we need juice, though,' and she smiled again. Just a little smile, but it was still a smile.

They walked round the shop, picking up bread, and sausages, and milk, and juice, and putting them in the trolley. Aunty Elizabeth had said she could choose things, but Izzy didn't. She remembered how Aunty Elizabeth was about the coffee.

Her mouth watered when they walked past the pizzas. She loved pizza! But Mum and Dad didn't like it, so they never had it at home. Maybe all adults didn't like pizza. Izzy couldn't help glancing at the cheese and tomato pizza – her favourite – on the shelf. Aunty Elizabeth saw, and stopped the trolley, right in the middle of the aisle.

'Would you like pizza?' Izzy didn't know what she was supposed to say, so she didn't say anything. 'I remember your mum doesn't like pizza,' said Aunty Elizabeth, thoughtfully. Izzy's head jerked upwards. That was the first time Aunty Elizabeth had mentioned Mum. Izzy's eyes filled with tears, and she blinked them away crossly. Aunty Elizabeth leaned over and put a cheese and tomato pizza in the trolley. 'That's my favourite. Now you put your favourite in, and one night this week we will have pizza.' Izzy looked at her aunt, then leaned across, took another cheese and tomato pizza from the shelf, and put it in the trolley. Aunty Elizabeth liked pizza! And their favourite was the same! Izzy looked at the two pizzas, side by side in the trolley, and felt a little bit HAPPY. The same happy as she'd felt when she found Gran's letters in Teddy.

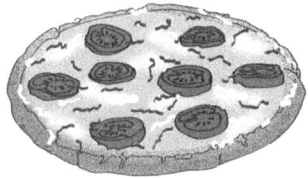

The letters! Izzy hugged her secret to herself as they finished shopping and waited in line to pay. To pass the time (of course they weren't talking), Izzy craned her neck to read the signs in the supermarket. She spotted the 'Pizza' sign.

When they drove back to Aunty Elizabeth's, the roof stayed down. They still didn't talk, but Izzy thought about the pizzas, and didn't mind so much.

Back at the flat, Aunty Elizabeth had some emails to send, and asked if Izzy would be alright on her own for a bit. Izzy managed not to **laugh**. Of course she would! She'd decided that it would be OK to open one more letter today. Gran would understand, and Izzy would save the rest, just as Gran had said.

When she got to her room, Izzy took the envelopes from Teddy's pocket and looked at them. Gran had put them in order, so Izzy picked up the next unopened one. She opened it and carefully took the folded paper from the envelope. Who was Gran's new friend?

Smoothing the letter out on the bed, she began to read:

Dear Izzy

I expect you're wondering about this friend of mine?

His name is Jesus, and Helen introduced me to him. You remember Helen, the lady who has moved into the house next door to me? You met her once, but only to say a quick hello.

Jesus is her friend, and she thought it would be nice if I met him, too.

The only Jesus I'd ever heard of was in Christmas stories, but I like meeting people's friends, as you know, so I said yes to Helen, and asked when I could meet him. She said, 'Now.' I looked around, but there was no one there! Maybe Helen is getting confused, I thought. 'Come into my house,' she said, 'and I'll introduce you.' Oh, he was in her house, that made sense. But I couldn't see anyone in the house, either! Helen made me a cup of tea, we sat at her kitchen table, and she began to tell me about her friend Jesus.

I was impatient to meet him, but thought maybe Helen wanted to tell me a bit about him first.

He wasn't born in a hospital, like you were. He was born in a stable, and he chose to be born! I asked Helen how someone could choose to be born. It doesn't make sense, does it? Helen said it was because Jesus is the Son of God – he knows everything. And it's because he knows everything that he chose to be born.

I was getting confused now, Izzy, so I sipped my tea and said nothing. But I began to wonder if Helen was talking about the Jesus in Christmas stories. And it turned out she was!

Do you remember last Christmas, Izzy, when you were in the nativity play at school? You were a shepherd, and had to wear a tea towel on your head! Well, Helen told me that the story about baby Jesus is not just a story, it's actually true! It really happened!

His Father God tried and tried for a long time to get people to know him – even by making the whole world! – but people didn't. So in the end, Jesus, who is the Son of God, the image of God, left heaven – which is where he lives – and came to live on earth for a while to show us what God is like.

So that's what these letters are about. My friend Jesus. I'm getting to know him and I'm looking forward to you getting to know him, too.

Don't read any more today, though – remember not to open all the letters at once!

Love from Gran

PS you can't see Jesus, but he is with you all the time.

Izzy read the letter all the way through three times, then slowly folded it back up and returned it to its envelope. She remembered that time she was a shepherd in the school play. The tea towel kept slipping off her head! But the story she'd been acting in actually happened?

And a new friend? Who was with her all the time? That would be nice, especially at the moment. Izzy looked around, but she couldn't see Jesus. Maybe Gran was wrong. Then she remembered that Gran had said she wouldn't see Jesus, but he was there. Maybe Gran was right. 'Hello, Jesus,' Izzy whispered, as an experiment. She felt uncomfortable. It was a bit **STRANGE** to think of Jesus being with her all the time.

Like Aunty Elizabeth. Izzy didn't know where that thought came from, but it was true. She was living in the same house as Aunty Elizabeth for now, and yet she didn't know her. All she knew was that she liked pizza! And white.

Maybe she could get to know Aunty Elizabeth as well as getting to know Jesus? But why should she? Aunty Elizabeth wouldn't speak to her mum! Izzy felt defensive.

She lay on the bed. What now? If only she was allowed a phone. All her friends had phones. Well, not all of them, but lots. Well, two. And they weren't really friends, they were just people in her year group. But still. Izzy had begged her mum for a phone, but her mum said not until she was 12. That was ages away.

Izzy turned her head and looked out of the window. Lots of buildings and no trees. She'd have to use her imagination. Imagine if all the buildings were trees, and all the windows were leaves. If windows were leaves, leaves must be windows. What if leaves really were windows? What would Izzy see if she could peep inside a leaf? Mr Simon had shown them leaves in biology, and they'd examined leaves through a microscope, looking at their cells. But what if there were things beyond the microscope? Things even a microscope didn't show. What if whole worlds existed inside a leaf, just like people's lives existed inside a house? Izzy began to imagine leaf people, tiny little figures, hurrying about inside a leaf. It was easier to imagine that than to think about how her own life would be with Aunty Elizabeth inside this white apartment.

'Izzy! Dinner!' Izzy snapped out of her daydream, jumped off the bed, and went to join her aunt in the kitchen.

Dinner was strange. Not the food, the food was OK, but Izzy usually talked to her mum and dad when they had dinner. They told each other about their days, or about anything. Izzy and Aunty Elizabeth ate in silence. A few times, Izzy thought Aunty Elizabeth was about to speak, but she never did. Maybe she didn't know what to say. Izzy didn't know what to say, either.

The clock on the wall **ticked** loudly. Izzy forced her food down, trying not to let her knife and fork make a noise when they touched her plate, and to chew without a sound.

When they'd finished eating, Aunty Elizabeth said that Izzy could go to her room if she wanted to. Izzy couldn't leave the table fast enough.

She lay on her bed and read a book for a bit, then she carried on with her daydream about leaf people. They probably talked to each other, in their leaf-language.

With a sigh that was more like a **HUFF**, Izzy picked up her Word Book. How could she sum up today in three words or less? She read what she'd written the night before. 'Rubbish' with an angry face. Maybe she'd just write the same again. She picked up her pen, then stopped. The *whole* day hadn't been rubbish. She wrote three words: Tears, Teddy, Pizza. In her mind, she wrote 'leaves' as well. That made four words, but one was invisible so Izzy thought it would be alright.

Later, Izzy got into bed. She didn't know if Aunty Elizabeth had gone to bed or not. The bed felt wrong, not like her own bed. And even though she'd switched the lights off, she could still see all the white. Or maybe she only saw it in her imagination. Either way, there was so much white, and it was so quiet here. Izzy's own house had cars driving past, and she wasn't used to going to sleep in silence. She shivered, and pulled Teddy close. At least he wasn't different.

Sunday

When Izzy woke up, she saw all the white and remembered where she was.

With a sigh that was more like a huff, she climbed out of bed, opened the white curtains, and **stared** out at the leaf-windows. She blinked in the morning light. The lives behind those leaves would all be great, she just knew it. They wouldn't have to do things like stay with an aunty they didn't know.

What about your words?

Izzy looked around. Where had that thought come from? The words were just a silly thing Mrs James was making them do. Last night's words floated through Izzy's mind, 'Tears, Teddy, Pizza'. Life was bad at the moment, but it wasn't all bad, she had to admit.

She looked at Teddy, sitting on her bed. The letters were in his pocket. Gran said Jesus was with her all the time. Maybe Jesus put the thought about her words in her head. Could he do that?

Izzy didn't know. She got back into bed, buried herself under the duvet, and stayed there.

Aunty Elizabeth was not sure what to do. She kept going to Izzy's bedroom door, standing outside it, and raising her hand to knock. But she never knocked. In the end she went and got on with some work. It wasn't as though she ever wanted Izzy to stay. She should be glad Izzy was staying in her room.

By about 11 a.m., Aunty Elizabeth had almost forgotten Izzy was there. Apart from hearing her walk to the bathroom, followed by the SLAM of the bedroom door, it was just like a normal Sunday.

Izzy buried deeper under the duvet. *Maybe I can stay here for the whole week*, she thought.

Aunty Elizabeth had been nervous about having Izzy to stay. She didn't know anything about children, and it was a long time since she'd been a child herself. If only she and her sister – Izzy's mum – hadn't had that falling out, maybe she would know Izzy, and have seen her lots of times, and they'd be good friends. But they didn't know each other, and they weren't friends.

Her phone buzzed. A text from her sister.

All fine here, Mum doing well, hope all good with you two.

Aunty Elizabeth felt a twinge of guilt. Things were good with her, but she had no idea about Izzy.

She sent the last email on her to-do list. It was midday, and there was no sound from the spare bedroom, so she reluctantly decided that she had better go and check on Izzy.

Standing again by the bedroom door, this time she KNOCKED. There was no answer. She knocked again. No answer. Torn between annoyance and worry, Aunty Elizabeth knocked, loudly, and opened the door. She couldn't see Izzy, all she could see was duvet.

'Time to get up, Izzy.'

When there was no response, she prodded the duvet.

After a few prods, Izzy's head emerged.

'What?'

'Come on, out of bed. We're going for a walk.'

Aunty Elizabeth didn't intend to say that, but she hadn't known what to say, and it slipped out.

'I'm not coming.' Izzy disappeared back under the duvet.

Aunty Elizabeth, who didn't even want to go for a walk, pulled the duvet off her niece. 'We're going for a walk. Get ready. We're going in ten minutes.'

Then she stood there, not taking her eyes off Izzy. Izzy could tell she meant it, and rolled off the bed with a huff that didn't even pretend to be a sigh.

Aunty Elizabeth heard it and ignored it.

Twelve minutes later, Izzy met her aunty by the front door. Without speaking, they left the flat.

Walking along beside Aunty Elizabeth, Izzy shoved her hands in her coat pockets, and kicked a stone along the pavement. She nearly trod on a leaf blowing along, but just in time she remembered about the little people inside, and stepped over it. Whatever the leaf people in that leaf were doing, it would be better than Izzy's day, and Izzy didn't want to spoil it for them.

Izzy and Aunty Elizabeth had to cross a busy road junction, and as they waited for the traffic lights to change, Izzy looked at the red-for-stop light, and thought about her mum's nail polish.

Crossing the road, they saw an ice-cream van. Aunty Elizabeth checked her watch.

'Oh, it's **ice cream o'clock**. Would you like an ice cream?'

She was desperate to do something so she could text her sister back and say,

Yes, things are good here.

'OK,' said Izzy.

At least she answered, thought Aunty Elizabeth.

They bought two cones, with chocolate flakes in. Izzy had chocolate sprinkles and raspberry sauce, too.

Aunty Elizabeth went to a little grassy area behind the van, and Izzy followed.

Sitting on the grass opposite each other, cross-legged, they began to eat their ice creams.

'What's ice cream o'clock?' Maybe the ice cream helped Izzy find her voice.

'Your grandad used to tell your mum and me when it was ice cream o'clock, and then he would buy us ice creams. It wasn't ice cream o'clock very often, though, only on special days.'

Izzy licked at a bit of ice cream dripping down her cone.

Aunty Elizabeth ate the last of her own ice cream, and leaned forward to pick a blade of grass. It was right next to a daisy. Izzy rolled her eyes. She would have picked the daisy. Why would anyone pick a blade of grass?

She watched as Aunty Elizabeth carefully put the grass between her thumbs, then lifted her hands to her mouth. She blew into her thumbs, and the grass made a BUZZING, *HUMMING* noise.

Izzy had never seen anyone do that before. Quickly finishing her ice cream, she picked a blade of grass and copied Aunty Elizabeth. No matter how hard she blew and blew and blew, no sound came out.

'Here, let me show you,' said Aunty Elizabeth, and helped Izzy until Izzy's grass made a noise. 'There you go!'

'I can't wait to show Mum this trick!' Izzy blew into her thumbs again, producing the grass-buzz.

Grass-buzz. That was the perfect way to describe it.

Aunty Elizabeth would never have guessed that a blade of grass might make things a bit better. She shook her head, and wondered if she would ever understand 11-year-olds.

'Your mum never could do this, however much she tried. She always asked me to do it, though. She liked the noise.'

As they walked home, Izzy was **thinking**. Aunty Elizabeth had talked about Mum today, and Izzy could tell they used to be good friends. What happened? Why didn't Mum and Aunty Elizabeth speak to each other anymore? What stopped them being friends?

'Aunty Elizabeth? Did you say ice cream o'clock only happens on special days?'

'Yes.'

'So is today a special day?'

Aunty Elizabeth glanced over. 'Do you think today is a special day?'

Izzy shrugged, but she didn't say no.

Back at the palatial flat, Izzy went to her room and flopped on the bed, but they both noted that she didn't slam the door this time.

It had been alright, going for a walk. Izzy was still angry about being stuck here with Aunty Elizabeth, but it had been alright. And it had been **amazing** ice cream!

Rolling off the bed, Izzy reached for her school bag. She had homework to do. She pulled her science textbook out of her bag, and a little notebook fell on the floor. It was her Word Book. Izzy dropped the textbook and read the words she'd already written.

'Rubbish'. Was that really only two days ago? It seemed like a million years had passed since then.

Yesterday's words: Tears, Teddy, Pizza.

Izzy began to think about what today's words would be, then forced herself to turn to page 27 in her science textbook and focus on the Periodic Table. There'd be time for Word Book later.

When it came to dinner time, Izzy was really hungry. They still didn't talk over dinner, but Izzy did mumble 'thank you' as she left the kitchen as soon as she could and went to her room.

She wasn't really sure what Aunty Elizabeth did in the evenings, and it seemed best to stay out of the way, but she didn't slam the door. Izzy was feeling better than she had this morning, and had remembered about Gran's letters. She took the next one out of Teddy's pocket, smoothed it out on the bed, and began to read:

Dear Izzy

I hope you're enjoying spending time with Jesus.

Izzy didn't know. She hadn't thought about Jesus today. Maybe she would start from now.

Today I am going to tell you about something that happened when Jesus was grown up.

Jesus was a great teacher, and crowds of people used to follow him around, to listen to him.

Can you imagine crowds of people following your teachers at school?

Everyone wanted to hear what Jesus had to say, and he told them about God, and how much God loved them.

Izzy put the letter down and picked up the letter from yesterday. She skimmed over it until she came to the bit that said Jesus is the Son of God, the image of God. If God loved people, then so did Jesus. *I'm a person,* thought Izzy. *So Jesus must **love me**. He's not just my friend, he actually loves me?* Izzy had never thought about Jesus loving her before.

She carried on reading:

> Where Jesus lived was hilly, it was not streets and houses like where you live, Izzy, so people would sit down on the hillside, and listen to Jesus.
>
> One day, Jesus went off on his own, but the crowds followed him, and when he saw them, he asked his disciples, who were his friends, 'Where can we buy food for all these people?'
>
> The disciples didn't know. There were thousands of people, and supermarkets hadn't been invented yet.

Izzy remembered the pizzas she and Aunty Elizabeth bought from the supermarket. Did Gran know they liked the same pizza?

But what happened to all this crowd of people?

> Eventually, one of Jesus' disciples, called Andrew, told Jesus he had found a boy who had a packed lunch with him. The packed lunch was five loaves and two fish.

That's not enough for thousands of people, thought Izzy, *even if they liked fish*. Izzy didn't like eating fish, it made her feel sick.

> Andrew thought there was not enough in the packed lunch, but Jesus disagreed and took the lunch from the boy. And the boy didn't mind! He just gave his lunch to Jesus!

Maybe fish was the boy's favourite. Izzy wondered if she would have given her pizza to Jesus. She wasn't sure.

> Jesus took the lunch, and thanked God for it, then gave it out to the crowd. It just kept coming, and there was enough food for everyone!
>
> Helen told me that is called a miracle, Izzy. When Jesus does amazing things like that, it's called a miracle.
>
> It is amazing, isn't it? Helen said Jesus provides everything we need.
>
> I'll tell you more about our friend Jesus next time.
>
> Love from Gran

Izzy climbed into bed.

Aunty Elizabeth seemed alright. Maybe. Izzy felt a bit less scared about staying here now, anyway. She couldn't wait to practise making grass-buzzes.

She reread the letter about Jesus, and how he fed the crowd. He **GAVE** them what they needed.

Before Jesus gave them the food, he thanked God for it.

Izzy had read a book where people did that before they ate a meal. It was called 'saying grace'. Once, Izzy had been at her friend's house for dinner, and was about to start eating when her friend's dad said, 'Shall we say grace?' Izzy had quickly put her knife and fork down, and Anna's dad had thanked God for their food.

If God made the whole world, like it said in Gran's letter, that meant everything in it. *So that means he made the food we eat*, thought Izzy. *And gave it to us, so that's like a present.* Izzy liked getting presents, and she always said thank you for them. But she'd never thanked Jesus for the present of food, even though she ate lots of food!

I've never thanked him, even though he's my friend. Well, he might be my friend. I want him to be. At least, I think I do.

Izzy folded the letter and put it back in Teddy's pocket.

She was nearly asleep, when she remembered her Word Book. Leaning over, she opened it and wrote: Duvet, Grass-buzz, Presents.

Tomorrow, she thought, as she drifted off to sleep, *tomorrow I will say grace . . .*

Monday

The next morning, when Izzy went through to the kitchen, Aunty Elizabeth was already there. 'Help yourself,' she said, pointing to some toast on the table. As Izzy slid into the seat opposite her aunt, she remembered about saying grace. She was so **nervous**! She tried to casually say, 'Shall we say grace before we eat?' but the words wouldn't come out of her mouth. It wasn't until Aunty Elizabeth was about to take a bite of toast and jam that Izzy blurted out, 'Shall we say grace?' Her cheeks felt as red as the strawberry jam.

Aunty Elizabeth slowly put down her toast.

Grace? She hadn't said grace for years. Where had Izzy got the idea of saying grace from?

'Well. Um. If you'd like to.' She bowed her head and closed her eyes.

Izzy saw the top of her aunt's head, and realized that she was supposed to say grace! She didn't know what to say. Aunty Elizabeth was waiting. Izzy felt her cheeks turn redder. The clock above the door ticked loudly. Izzy panicked. *Jesus! Help! I want to thank you but I don't know what to say!* It was as though he told her: 'Just say thank you.'

She'd talked to Jesus! And he'd ANSWERED her!

Izzy gulped, and took a deep breath.

'Jesus

Thank you for this food that you have given to us as a present.

Amen.'

Phew, she thought, slumping back in her chair. *I did it.*

Aunty Elizabeth picked up her toast again. She was thoughtful as she bit into it, and watched her niece, who had straightened up and was busy buttering a piece of toast. Izzy seemed different.

'I spoke to your mum on the phone last night.' Aunty Elizabeth took a sip of coffee. 'She sends her love and says your gran is doing as well as can be expected, and is looking forward to their holiday. They are going today.'

What did 'as well as can be expected' mean? But Izzy didn't ask out loud, she just nodded. If only she was allowed a phone, she could ask Mum herself. She didn't dare ask to use Aunty Elizabeth's phone.

After breakfast, Aunty Elizabeth needed to go to her office and Izzy needed to go to school. School was close to the flat, and Izzy could walk there.

Say it, she silently begged her aunty, *say you'll meet me after school, just like Amy's aunty does.* But Aunty Elizabeth gave Izzy a door key, and told her to let herself in after school.

As Izzy put the key carefully in her purse, she realised she was secretly relieved. She wanted Aunty Elizabeth to meet her, but at the same time she didn't want her to. What was all that about?

Izzy picked up her bag and walked away from the flat.

Her first lesson of the day was cooking, and they made bread. As she made the dough for the bread, Izzy imagined that she was the little boy who gave Jesus his picnic, and the five rolls were ones she made herself. She would give her lunch to Jesus, even if it was pizza, she decided.

Next was maths, followed by geography, then art, then lunchtime. Izzy went to the usual place where she met her friends, by the long grass at the bottom corner of the playing field. In other words, as far away as they could go from school! The rest of the gang were already there.

'Hi, Izzy! How's your gran?'

'Lucy said you're staying with your aunty?'

The questions kept coming.

'Is it the aunty no one talks to?'

'Is it a nightmare having to stay with her?'

'Gran is doing as well as can be expected,' said Izzy, repeating what Aunty Elizabeth had said earlier.

The gang nodded. She could see that none of them know what that meant, either.

'What about your aunty?' Jo offered her bag of crisps round. 'What's she like?'

They all knew Izzy would not have wanted to go and stay at Aunty Elizabeth's.

'She's OK, actually,' said Izzy, crunching a salt and vinegar crisp.

Izzy told them about the pizzas, and the ice cream, and the grass-buzz noise. She was too shy to tell them about grace, though, or that Jesus was helping her.

'She does sound OK,' said Lucy.

'Can you show us how to do the grass-buzz thing?' asked Jo.

Izzy nodded and bent to pick a blade of grass. As she did, she saw Kelly sitting **ALONE**, a little distance away. Kelly was in some of the same classes as Izzy. She had only come to the school about two weeks ago. Kelly kept watching Izzy's gang, looking away if anyone noticed.

Izzy remembered Gran's letter. Jesus really cared about people, and noticed them. He saw that they were hungry.

Jesus would notice Kelly.

'I'll be back in a minute.' Izzy jumped up and walked over to where Kelly was sitting.

The rest of the gang frowned, looking at each other. Where was Izzy going?

Izzy flopped down beside Kelly. 'Hi.'

Kelly looked surprised. 'Um, hi.'

Izzy looked at the crutches lying on the grass beside Kelly. She reached out to touch one, then changed her mind.

'Why do you need crutches?'

Kelly didn't say anything, but she moved the crutches nearer to her.

Izzy leaned back on her hands.

'What do you think of this school?'

Kelly shrugged. 'It's alright.'

'You'll soon get used to it. I know it's massive, but you'll learn your way around.'

Kelly just shrugged.

'Are you OK?'

'Yes.' Kelly looked away as she said it. 'No. I miss my old school, and my friends there.'

'Why did you move schools?' Izzy thought she should already know this.

'Because my dad got a new job. I was going to stay with my grandad until the end of the year, so I could stay at the same school, but then he got poorly, and I had to move when Dad did.'

'What's wrong with your grandad?'

'I don't know. Dad won't tell me.'

'Same with me and my gran. No one will tell me what's wrong.'

'It's hard, isn't it?' said Kelly, in a small voice.

Izzy nodded. This was the first time anyone had understood.

The two girls looked at each other. Izzy was thinking about the little boy and his packed lunch. It was only small, but he still gave it. He just wanted to help.

Izzy wanted to help Kelly, but she didn't know how. The grass tickled her, and she thought of something she could do! Jesus must have told her. 'Thank you,' she whispered inside, as she sat up and picked a blade of grass.

Twirling it between her fingers, she asked, 'Do you know how to make grass buzz?'

Kelly shook her head.

Izzy showed Kelly and Kelly picked some grass and tried it herself. Izzy's gang heard and came over. They sat down, and soon they were making grass-buzzes, too, and everyone was laughing at the funny noise.

It looked as though the gang had a new member!

After school, as she walked through the gates, Izzy saw Amy climbing into her aunty's car.

Izzy SHRUGGED. Whatever. There was no point looking for Aunty Elizabeth's car. Checking she had the door key in her purse, Izzy set off to walk back to Aunty Elizabeth's.

She let herself in. Aunty Elizabeth must still be at work. Izzy went to her bedroom, stopping to get some juice on the way. There was Teddy on the bed. Izzy lay down beside him, bending her knees.

She turned her head and looked out of the window. What was happening behind the leaf windows today? She found it more difficult to imagine than before.

Sitting up, Izzy took a couple of swigs of juice, then felt in Teddy's pocket. She wouldn't read today's letter yet, but she would reread yesterday's.

As she read, she kept noticing similarities between her day and the story about Jesus. She supposed that made sense, since it was the same Jesus!

That boy who gave his picnic probably didn't think he had much to give, but he just did what he could do, and he really helped.

Izzy had just done what she could do, with the grass-buzz, and it had made a big difference. Now Kelly had friends at school, including Izzy.

Jesus had been **glad** when the boy gave his lunch to help the crowd. 'Was he glad when I helped Kelly?' Izzy wondered. She thought he was.

A key turned in the lock, and the door to the flat opened. Aunty Elizabeth must be home. *What if things were different now?* Izzy decided to stay in her room and do her homework.

She had history and maths. Izzy was good at history, and she really liked her teacher, which made lessons fun.

Maths was different. Her teacher was scary for a start, always glaring through her glasses. And Izzy could never remember the equations and things. If Mrs McDonald picked on her to answer a question, Izzy panicked.

She decided to leave her maths until last. Mum always said it is best to get the worst thing out of the way first, but Izzy wasn't so sure. Not today, anyway.

Thinking of Mum made Izzy feel sad. She wondered how Gran was, and if they were missing her.

History homework was a project about the Romans, and soon Izzy was absorbed.

She finished the project, and was about to start on her maths when she heard Aunty Elizabeth calling her for dinner.

Jumping up from where she'd been lying on the floor, Izzy went to join Aunty Elizabeth. Maths could wait.

Homework

Izzy sat down at her usual place, and Aunty Elizabeth sat opposite her.

'Are you going to say grace?'

A look of surprise crossed Izzy's face.

Aunty Elizabeth was a little surprised herself.

All day she had been thinking about Izzy saying grace at breakfast. It wasn't that Aunty Elizabeth didn't believe in God. She never really gave him much thought, except for going to church at Christmas. She always liked seeing the children in a nativity play, acting out the story of Jesus being born, but Izzy didn't seem to think it was a story. She talked to Jesus as though he was alive right now. As though he was **real**. What if he was real?

Izzy cleared her throat, pulling Aunty Elizabeth from her thoughts.

'Jesus,

Thank you for this food.

Amen.'

'Amen,' said Aunty Elizabeth softly, looking at Izzy's bowed head.

Izzy's head shot up, and she looked at Aunty Elizabeth. She'd said Amen. It was as though they had been talking to Jesus **together**! Saying grace had been easier, this time, too. *I must be getting used to talking to Jesus.*

Picking up her knife and fork, she began to eat.

'Today I showed someone how to do grass-buzz.'

'That's great!'

'Yeah.'

It was not much of a conversation, but it was better than not talking at all.

After dinner, Izzy helped with the washing up. She didn't like washing up, but at least it meant she didn't have to go and do her maths homework yet.

'Do you have any homework?' asked Aunty Elizabeth, wiping a plate clean. Izzy nearly dropped the plate she was drying. Had Aunty Elizabeth read her mind? That was scary!

Aunty Elizabeth saw, and wondered if she shouldn't have asked. She didn't know. She'd never had an 11-year-old staying before.

'I have history and maths. I've done the history, and I'll try to do the maths when we've washed up.'

'Do you like maths?'

Izzy pulled a face. How could anyone like maths?

'Izzy, do you know what I do for my job?'

Izzy knew Aunty Elizabeth worked in an office. Mum had told her that, but Izzy had no idea what Aunty Elizabeth did in the office.

'No.'

'I'm an accountant. I do maths every day! I couldn't help much with history, I was always terrible at history, but I can help with maths. Why don't you bring your homework into the sitting room? Let's see if we can work it out together.'

Izzy wasn't sure. She was so bad at maths, no one could help her. She was **EMBARRASSED** about Aunty Elizabeth seeing how stupid she was. And what if Aunty Elizabeth couldn't help her? She seemed so sure she could, and she might get cross if it didn't work.

Aunty Elizabeth saw the doubt on Izzy's face.

'Come on!' she nudged her niece. 'We can do this! Go and fetch your books, I'll meet you in the sitting room in a couple of minutes.'

When Izzy arrived, carrying her maths books, Aunty Elizabeth was already there. There was a cup of coffee, a glass of juice and a bowl of chocolate buttons on the coffee table. Izzy sat down.

'Right,' said Aunty Elizabeth, 'before we start, it is absolutely essential that we have some chocolate,' and she put a button in her mouth. Izzy did the same. They both liked chocolate as well as pizza! Maths homework was better already with Aunty Elizabeth!

For the next hour, the two of them worked on Izzy's homework, eating chocolate, heads close together as Aunty Elizabeth explained how to solve the problems.

She was very **patient**. She didn't make Izzy feel stupid, she just explained things again and again, until Izzy understood. When they reached the end of the homework, Izzy really understood it. She didn't think she'd ever like maths the way she liked history, but it was good to understand it.

'Thank you,' she said to Aunty Elizabeth.

And thank you, Jesus, she added inside. He was there too.

Izzy recalled the letter, about the boy giving his lunch to help people, and how Jesus had used it.

Izzy had given Kelly the grass-buzz lesson, and now Kelly had friends and was happier.

Aunty Elizabeth had given Izzy help with maths, and now Izzy felt a bit more confident.

Thank you, Jesus.

Thinking about the letter reminded Izzy that there was another one waiting to be opened. The letters were still her secret; she wasn't ready to tell anyone about them yet.

After saying goodnight to Aunty Elizabeth, Izzy went to her room and reached for Teddy.

The first letter had been about getting to know Jesus.

The second one had been about helping others.

Having Jesus as a friend was really good.

What would the third letter be about?

Izzy took the little envelope from Teddy's pocket, and smoothed it out on the bed.

Dear Izzy
Helen told me about another time Jesus was in a crowd. He was so popular! Just like you at school!

Am I popular? wondered Izzy. *I suppose I do have my friends, but I don't know if that makes me popular.* She made a mental note to ask Gran why she thought Izzy was popular. *Probably because she's my gran!*

Izzy carried on reading:

Jesus was walking along in the middle of a massive crowd. People were everywhere, squashing into each other. Suddenly, Jesus stopped walking. I can just imagine people all bumping into each other!

Izzy giggled, remembering when she was in primary school a few years ago. The teacher had told the class to form a line and walk across the playground. Jamie had been in front, and had suddenly stopped because he needed to tie his shoelace. Everyone behind had bumped into the person in front of them!

Then Jesus asked a strange question: 'Who touched me?'

Jesus' disciples said, 'It could have been anyone. We are all bumping into each other here!'

They had a fair point, in that packed crowd.

But Jesus said, 'No, someone definitely touched me.'

And then he just stood there, waiting.

In the end a woman said, 'It was me.'

Apparently, she had been poorly for twelve years. She kept bleeding. No one wanted to talk to her, or even be near her.

Twelve years? That was longer than Izzy had been alive! Izzy knew that it is dangerous to lose a lot of blood. Once a month for a few days is alright; they'd learned about that happening to girls, in PSHE. It was called a period, or menstruating. It was normal.

But if this woman had been bleeding for twelve years, she would have lost a lot of blood. She was probably amelic. No, amelic wasn't right. An-something. Anomy? Anaemic. That was it, the lady was probably anaemic, which would make her really tired.

> It was brave of her to go into that crowd, Izzy, but she was determined to get to Jesus, because she thought he could help her. She was a bit scared to ask him, though.

Izzy knew that feeling! She'd been scared about having Aunty Elizabeth help her with her maths, but it had all worked out well. She hoped the woman had been brave enough to ask Jesus.

> So she thought if she touched Jesus' clothes, that might be enough. And do you know what? It was! As soon as she touched his clothes, the bleeding stopped. Isn't that amazing?

Izzy wondered what the opposite of anaemic was . . .

The woman turned around to try to sneak back through the crowd, which is when Jesus stopped, and all the people bumped into each other, and she had to say, 'It was me that touched you.'

Jesus looked at her.

Can you imagine how nervous she must have felt, Izzy? Jesus looking right at her, with all the people crowding around?

Jesus said to her, 'Go in peace.'

Helen said that was special. No one else had really noticed her, they just found her annoying and didn't like her, but Jesus took time to notice her.

Helen said Jesus notices everyone.

Love from Gran

Izzy changed into her pyjamas and climbed into bed. She was thinking about the letter. She felt sorry for the woman. It must be **HORRIBLE** to have everyone find you annoying. Sometimes Izzy herself was annoying. Mum got annoyed when her bedroom was messy! But Mum wasn't annoyed with her all the time, and she knew Mum liked her. This woman annoyed everyone, and no one liked her.

'I'm glad you noticed her, Jesus.'

Do you know anyone like the woman? Izzy knew that was Jesus. She was becoming used to 'hearing in her heart'.

She thought about it. Did she know anyone like the woman? No, she didn't think so.

I think you do.

Izzy tried to picture people she knew. She visualized school, and her classmates. A girl popped into her mind.

Suzy! Suzy annoyed EVERYONE and no one liked her. She was so mean, and Izzy always tried to avoid her. Once, when they were playing netball, Suzy had deliberately tripped Izzy up, and she missed the ball. Or what about in geography, when Jo had started to sit down at her desk and Suzy had sneaked up and pulled her chair away. Jo had ended up falling on the floor! She had really hurt herself.

'It's best if I stay away from Suzy, Jesus.'

Is it?

Is it? Izzy mused, as she lay down to sleep. *I wish it was, but I don't think Jesus thinks it is . . .*

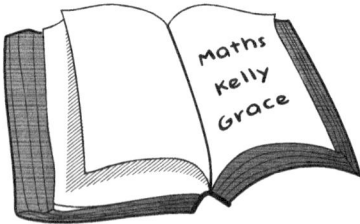

She sat up again, remembering her Word Book. Casting her mind back over the day, she chose: Maths, Kelly, Grace.

Lying down again, and curled up under her duvet, Izzy realized that there were no negative words this time. Even maths! Despite a few wobbles, overall the day had been good.

Tuesday

When Izzy went into the kitchen on Tuesday morning, Aunty Elizabeth was already there. They sat at the table together, and Izzy was about to say grace, when she heard:

'Jesus,

Thank you for this food.

Amen.'

'Amen,' said Izzy.

Aunty Elizabeth picked up her spoon and began to eat her cornflakes. She looked a bit embarrassed, but she also looked **happy**. *Was Jesus becoming Aunty Elizabeth's friend, too?* wondered Izzy, as she ate her breakfast. She hoped so.

'Aunty Elizabeth?'

'Yes?' Aunty Elizabeth took a sip of coffee.

'There's this girl at school called Suzy.'

Aunty Elizabeth didn't say anything, but she kept looking at Izzy. Izzy carried on:

'She's really mean, apart from to her friends. She trips people over and pushes them. Everyone is scared of her. She's a bully. Did I mention that she's mean?'

Izzy waited for Aunty Elizabeth to agree with her and say that Suzy did sound mean.

But she didn't.

'Do you know why she bullies people?'

'Because she's mean.'

Didn't Aunty Elizabeth hear her the first time?

'Are you sure she's mean, Izzy?'

Why would Aunty Elizabeth doubt it? Izzy was **confused**. Unless . . .

'Do you know Suzy?'

Aunty Elizabeth looked at the pink polish on her nails. 'Sort of.'

Sort of? Aunty Elizabeth was making no sense at all.

'Izzy, I used to be Suzy.'

Now Izzy was even more confused. Had Aunty Elizabeth changed her name or something?

Aunty Elizabeth corrected herself.

'I mean I used to be *like* Suzy.'

Izzy's mouth dropped open. Aunty Elizabeth used to be mean?

'Is that why you and Mum don't get on?' The words were out before Izzy could stop them. She put her hand over her mouth, wishing she hadn't said that.

A flicker of something passed over Aunty Elizabeth's eyes. Aunty Elizabeth was not going to answer her. Izzy started to leave the table, when Aunty Elizabeth shook her head.

'No. I was like Suzy when I was at school.'

Izzy sat back down. *So Mum and Aunty Elizabeth didn't fall out while they were still at school?* Interesting.

'I was the one who tripped people over, and pushed them. People were scared of me. I was a *BULLY*.'

Izzy looked at her aunt, not sure what to say. She'd been a bully? Izzy couldn't quite get her head around this new information. She repeated the question Aunty Elizabeth asked about Suzy.

'Why did you bully people?'

'Because I was unhappy.'

'Oh, well this is different. Suzy's not unhappy. She's just mean.'

'How do you know she's not unhappy, Izzy?'

'Because she lives in a big house, and always has the best clothes, and she wears black make-up – only the cool girls do that – and she doesn't care what people think of her, and her friends all think she's great.'

Aunty Elizabeth began to clear the breakfast things off the table.

'Izzy, all those things you just said are "outside" things. What about **inside**?'

'Inside?'

'I mean Suzy's feelings and thoughts. Is she happy inside?' Izzy didn't know.

'Were *you* happy inside?'

'I – oh, look at the time! You'd better hurry, or you'll be late for school.'

Will you meet me after school? Izzy didn't say it aloud, even as she realized that now she definitely did want Aunty Elizabeth to meet her. Instead, she fetched her bag, put her coat on and waved goodbye.

As she walked to school, Izzy was thinking. Aunty Elizabeth had asked if Suzy was unhappy. If Suzy was unhappy, which Izzy doubted, no one noticed. The woman in Gran's letter had been unhappy, but no one noticed her, either.

Jesus noticed her, though. Did Jesus notice Suzy? Izzy knew he did; he noticed everyone. Izzy knew that her friend Jesus wanted her to notice Suzy, too.

The idea scared her.

I'll help, she heard in her heart.

'Thank you,' she whispered to Jesus, taking a deep breath as she turned in at the school gate.

Izzy decided to find Suzy at break time, just as class finished, before Suzy had time to go off and be cool with her gang, but Jesus had other plans. As Izzy walked past the bike sheds to the left of the gate, there was Suzy! And she was on her own.

Izzy GULPED.

Jesus, please help.

She walked over to where Suzy was standing. Suzy looked up from her mobile phone. *She* would *be allowed one*. Izzy pushed that thought from her mind.

'What do *you* want?' Suzy sneered. Her face had the usual hard look, but Izzy saw the tears in her eyes before Suzy quickly blinked them away.

Izzy took a deep breath. 'I wondered how you're doing?'

She could see Suzy was suspicious. 'What? Why would you ask that? Get lost!'

Izzy didn't move.

'What are you hanging around for?' Suzy looked back at her phone.

Izzy wanted to run away, but something helped her stay.

'I just want to know if you're OK.'

'Course I am. Why wouldn't I be? I'm fine . . .'

Suzy trailed off. Izzy didn't seem to be joking, but Suzy didn't know what to say. Of course she wasn't OK. She was never OK these days, but she was good at **PRETENDING** to be. Wasn't she? So why did Izzy ask if she was OK? No one ever asked her that. Suzy thought about the message she'd just read on her phone, telling her that her brother had walked two steps. Everything was always about her brother. Tears pricked Suzy's eyes again. Mum was so busy with him, she never had time for Suzy. When Jack was born, it was as though Suzy stopped existing. 'Suzy, can you fetch a nappy for Jack' or 'Sorry, Suzy, I can't talk now, I need to look after Jack'. Suzy knew she had become mean at school, but at least it made people notice her. She existed at school. Not like at home, when no one cared about her. She couldn't remember the last time anyone asked her how she was.

Izzy looked nervous. She was biting her nails, but she didn't walk away. Maybe she **was** interested? Suzy doubted it, but she decided to be honest.

'No. I'm not OK.'

Izzy hadn't expected that. What now?

She thought back to the woman who had touched Jesus' clothes. What did Jesus do? He noticed her and he talked to her. *How can I notice Suzy now, Jesus?*

Talk to her.

Talk to her. Right.

'Um . . .'

Suzy grabbed Izzy's arm and pulled her at a run behind the bike shed. Izzy was really 𝕊𝕮𝔸ℝ𝔼𝔻 now.

'Sorry!' said Suzy, breathlessly. 'It's just I saw my gang and I don't want them coming over.'

Izzy tried to speak, but she was breathing hard, too. Their breathing slowed, and the two girls looked at each other, laughing.

Izzy dropped her backpack and sat down with her back to the wall.

Suzy sat down beside her.

Laughing together had made Izzy relax. 'Why are you not OK?'

Suzy looked up at the sky, watching the clouds floating by, and told Izzy about Jack.

Aunty Elizabeth had been right! Suzy was unhappy.

'Izzy, do you think I'm mean?'

Izzy looked at the ground.

'Come on, you can tell me the truth, Izzy. I can take it.'

'Well, yes, you are a bit.'

'Everyone thinks that. But I'm not mean. Not really. It's just everyone ignores me if I'm not being loud, and naughty, and mean.'

What? Suzy was mean because otherwise people would ignore her?

'You're not being mean now, and I'm not ignoring you, am I?'

'No, but – ' Suzy paused. 'Why are you talking to me? Why are you being nice? I made Jo fall on the floor yesterday, and Jo is your friend.'

Izzy was surprised Suzy even remembered doing that, she was always doing mean things. But now Izzy knew Suzy didn't like doing those things.

Jesus had told the woman to go in peace. Peace meant not being worried inside. Suzy was worried inside.

Izzy thought about the windows she could see from the bedroom at Aunty Elizabeth's. The windows she pretended were leaves on trees. She liked pretending, but she would only know what really happened behind the windows if she could look. A bit like Suzy. She only knew what Suzy was feeling inside because she'd taken time to look.

Thank you, Jesus, for teaching me to look.

'Suzy, you don't have to be mean, you know. You're nice just as you are. And I don't think you are mean really.'

Suzy was relieved. Someone had noticed the real her. But how come? How come Izzy had taken time for her? Suzy was about to ask, when they heard the school bell. Time for class.

Izzy stood up and brushed the dust from her skirt. She looked down at Suzy. 'You coming?'

'In a minute.'

Suzy watched Izzy walk away. Before she turned the corner, Izzy looked back and waved. Suzy waved too.

Maybe Izzy was right that people would still notice her if she stopped being mean. Suzy wasn't sure. Stopping would be really hard, but she knew she didn't like being mean. Izzy had been **BRAVE** to talk to her, and the thought made Suzy wrinkle her nose in disgust. People shouldn't need to pluck up courage just to talk to her!

Standing up, Suzy picked up her bag and followed in the same direction as Izzy.

As she walked through the door of the geography room, Suzy saw her gang in their usual place in the corner at the back. They always made sure they sat at the back. Sometimes the teacher made them move, but not always. On the other side of the room, Suzy saw Izzy and her friends.

Suzy began to swagger over to her mates, and people moved out of her way. She usually felt powerful when they did that, but today she didn't feel so good about it.

Izzy's words rang in her mind: 'You don't have to be mean, you know.'

I don't have *to be mean . . .*

Suzy changed direction and went over to where Izzy and her friends were. They all stopped talking and stared at Suzy, with a mixture of amazement and fear, but mostly fear. What was Suzy doing there?

Suzy looked at Jo.

'Sorry about yesterday with the chair,' she muttered.

'Er . . .' Jo didn't know what to say. She wouldn't have been more surprised if Suzy had turned bright green! Just then the teacher arrived, and everyone quickly scrambled to sit at their tables. Jo passed a piece of paper to Izzy:

How weird was that?! Wonder what's got into Suzy????

Izzy wrote back:

Maybe we should give her a chance?

Jo quickly scribbled on the paper:

what?!?!?!

Before Izzy could reply, Mr Forrest clapped his hands and told everyone to focus. Mr Forrest had a great name for a geography teacher! Izzy tried to concentrate on ice caps melting because of climate change, and how that was not good, but she kept imagining Suzy as a mountain, with all the hard bits *MELTING* off. Would they melt off? Hopefully. Maybe it was a sort of climate change, but a good one!

Afternoon Off

Izzy didn't see much of Suzy for the rest of the day, but she saw her across the playing field after school, walking towards the gate to go home. Suzy gave her a little wave and, as Izzy waved back, she whispered, 'Jesus, please let Suzy's mum have some time for her tonight.'

Was it OK to ask Jesus things like that? Izzy thought so; Jesus was interested in everyone.

She turned left out of the gate and set off towards Aunty Elizabeth's flat, walking past Amy as she did. She half-heartedly looked for Aunty Elizabeth's car, but didn't really expect it to be there. It wasn't. Izzy was looking forward to seeing Aunty Elizabeth, though, so she could tell her about Suzy.

She let herself in and closed the door of the flat behind her. A bag and shoes were in the hallway. Aunty Elizabeth was already home. 'Gran! Something's happened to Gran.' Pulling off her coat, Izzy DASHED into the sitting room.

'What's happened? What's wrong?'

Aunty Elizabeth was sitting on the sofa, flicking through a magazine. She looked up at her flustered niece. 'Nothing's happened.'

'Oh,' said Izzy in relief. No bad news about Gran. 'It's just that you're home early.'

'I know. I took the afternoon off. We have a conversation from this morning to finish.'

Izzy stared. Aunty Elizabeth had remembered, and was going to tell her about why she used to be like Suzy?

Aunty Elizabeth couldn't remember the last time she took an afternoon off.

'I'll be back in a minute.' Izzy went and dumped her school bag on her bed. When she returned to the sitting room, she saw that Aunty Elizabeth had made her a drink and put out a bowl of chocolate buttons.

Aunty Elizabeth patted the seat beside her on the sofa. 'Come and sit down, Izzy.'

Izzy sat down, helping herself to some chocolate.

Aunty Elizabeth had been wondering where to start, and decided to just launch in.

'I wasn't always a bully. In junior school I got on with everyone. I had lots of friends. I was happy.'

'What changed?'

'School changed. I moved up to secondary school, and none of my friends went to the same one as me.'

A bit like Kelly, thought Izzy. She must remember to tell Aunty Elizabeth about Kelly.

'I was lonely. I had no one to talk to, and everyone just ignored me and went off with their friends. I used to sit on my own, and eat lunch on my own, and walk home on my own. I was **miserable**, Izzy.

'One day, I was walking down the corridor when someone walked into me. They only did it by accident, but I shouted at them: "Oi, watch where you're going!" I never normally said anything, but that day I was feeling really sad and missing my friends, and I snapped. The person mumbled "sorry" and walked off. I carried on down the corridor and further down I saw a group of girls, watching me. "The Girlz" they were called. Everyone was scared of them. I never spoke to them, and they only spoke to me to be mean. But this time, as I walked past, Emma – the gang leader – said, "Hi! There's a spare place on our table if you want to sit with us at lunch."

'All morning, I was thinking about it. The Girlz were not very nice, but it would be great not to sit on my own at lunchtime, and it felt good not to be ignored. So I sat with them at lunchtime, and then every lunchtime after that. I started hanging out with them more and more, and soon I was bullying people just like they did.'

'And that was because you were ignored, and no one noticed you?'

'Yes. And then everyone thought I really was mean and even though I never fitted in, I didn't know how to stop. And then I didn't want to stop, because people didn't ignore me when I was mean. And that's why I was a bully.'

Izzy took some more chocolate. She couldn't think of anything to say. She'd never realized that bullies might be the way they were because they were **UNHAPPY**.

'Did you talk to Suzy today?'

'Yeah, and you were right. She bullies people because she's unhappy at home. Everyone ignores her since her brother came along. I didn't ignore her today, and do you know what? I think she's quite nice, really.'

'Well done, Izzy,' Aunty Elizabeth put her arm around Izzy for a quick hug.

Izzy wondered if she dared ask. 'Would it be OK if – '

Aunty Elizabeth said, 'Would you like it if – '

Laughing, they both stopped talking and waited for the other to finish.

'You first.' Izzy popped another chocolate button into her mouth.

'Would you like it if Suzy came here with you after school one day?'

That was exactly what Izzy had been going to say! She'd like Suzy to meet Aunty Elizabeth.

Izzy nodded. 'Shall I see if she can come on Thursday? Is that OK? Will we need to get more pizza?'

Aunty Elizabeth laughed again. 'Yes, Thursday is fine. But Izzy, we won't be having pizza. That's just for us this time.'

Izzy was surprised by how good that made her feel.

Aunty Elizabeth was surprised that she'd invited another 11-year-old round!

Later, in bed, Izzy talked with Jesus about her day:

'It's been a good day. Thank you for helping me. I was really nervous about speaking to Suzy, but you gave me **courage**. I'm not so scared of her now. I hope she can come on Thursday.'

Then she turned out the light.

She quickly turned it back on again.

The letters! How could she have forgotten?

As she undid the zip on Teddy's pocket, she thought back.

The first letter had been about getting to know Jesus. Izzy was getting to know him, and she was getting to know Aunty Elizabeth, too.

The second one had been about giving what we can to help others. Izzy thought back to Kelly and the grass-buzz. She was really glad she'd been able to help Kelly, and now Kelly was becoming a good friend.

The third letter had been about **noticing** people. Izzy noticed Suzy today, and she'd learned that there was more to Aunty Elizabeth than it seemed.

Why had Aunty Elizabeth been sent to a different school from her friends? And why had Mum and Aunty Elizabeth fallen out? Maybe Izzy would be brave enough to ask Aunty Elizabeth one day. But for now, it was time to open Gran's next letter! Izzy carefully opened the little envelope, pulled out the paper, and began to read.

Dear Izzy
Helen told me something else about Jesus. It involves trees – I know you like trees!

Izzy smiled as she thought about all the houses outside her window being trees, and the windows being leaves. No one else knew that lives happen in the leaves.

One day, when Jesus was walking along, he suddenly stopped, looked up into a tree, and said, 'Come on, come down,

I'm coming back to your house with you.'
I thought Jesus must have gone a bit
strange, talking to trees but, would you
believe it, a little man suddenly peered
through the leaves and began to climb
down.

Izzy's eyes opened wide. Jesus knew a life was happening behind leaves, too!

Apparently, the man, who was called
Zacchaeus, was there because he was too
small to see over the crowd. It's probably
a good thing he was hidden, too. No one
liked him, which was fair enough of
them because he stole their money.

But Jesus noticed him, and just said,
'I'm coming to your house.' I said to Helen
that maybe Jesus didn't know the man
stole things, but Helen said he did. She
said Jesus just wanted to be a friend to
Zacchaeus, even though no one else did.

Love from Gran

P.S. After he met Jesus, Zacchaeus felt bad
about stealing, and gave people what he
owed them. Actually, he gave them more
than he owed!

Izzy put the letter away in Teddy's pocket and lay down in bed. Reading the letter had made her **HOMESICK** for Mum and Dad and Gran. She wanted to see them. If only she had a phone. Izzy rubbed her eyes. It wasn't fair.

Sniffling, Izzy turned off the light, and hugged Teddy. Teddy smelled like Gran's house. Fresh tears filled Izzy's eyes.

To stop herself thinking about Mum and Dad and Gran for a bit, she thought about the letter. She was glad Jesus was her friend. She thought about her other friends. Jo, her best friend, who made her laugh. Lucy, who always knew the best music. Lucy's uncle played drums for a band in China; he was really famous. Kelly, who Izzy already felt she'd known forever. Suzy . . . Izzy stopped. It felt weird to call Suzy a friend. She'd never have thought she'd name Suzy in her list of friends! It was early days, but she was beginning to. *Thank you, Jesus.* Izzy carried on picturing people from school, until her thoughts came to an abrupt stop again. Katy.

When Katy was at school, she was just there in the background. She was really quiet, and didn't talk to anyone. Izzy didn't think she had ever spoken to her. Katy tried not to even look at anyone. Izzy couldn't remember anything about Katy, except that she had brown hair.

Or was it blonde? Whichever, it was definitely long, and Katy always had it hanging over her face. No one noticed Katy.

Izzy couldn't remember the last time she even saw her. Katy hadn't been at school for a while.

Would Jesus notice Katy? The letter had said he noticed people hidden in trees, so Izzy guessed he'd notice people who hid behind their hair at school.

Yes, I would. Izzy smiled at that; she was getting to know her friend Jesus.

Maybe tomorrow, if Katy was back at school, Izzy would try to notice her a bit more.

She felt a rush of homesickness again. Was it alright to tell Jesus?

'Jesus? I'm feeling sad.'

I know.

Izzy settled down to sleep. She was still sad, and it felt good to know that Jesus knew. She could be **honest** with him.

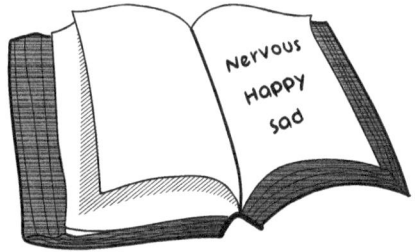

Just as she was falling asleep, she remembered her Word Book. Izzy couldn't be bothered. 'I'll write my words in the morning.' Her words were: Nervous, Happy, Sad. She'd been all those things today.

Wednesday

The next morning, Izzy was still sad. She missed her parents. She'd never been away from Mum for this long before. She wanted to **HIDE** under the duvet all day. Maybe she should tell Aunty Elizabeth that she was not very well. She remembered the times she'd tried that with Mum when she didn't want to go to school. It never worked. Izzy dragged herself out of bed and washed and dressed. As she did, she saw Teddy from the corner of her eye. Could she . . .? No. She made herself look away. She was only opening one letter a day, at bedtime. But Teddy kept coming into view, and Izzy couldn't resist. She wanted to feel closer to Gran, so she leaned over, reached for Teddy, and pulled a letter from his pocket.

Settling cross-legged on the bed, she began to read.

Dear Izzy

I learned something totally new about Jesus today. I was telling Helen about how chopping onions always makes me cry.

You remember, don't you?

Izzy nodded. Whenever Gran chopped onions, Izzy knew to have tissues ready.

Helen said it's OK to cry, and that Jesus did. I asked if Jesus chopped onions, too? Helen laughed, and said she doubted it! He cried because he was sad.

Only Gran would ask if Jesus chopped onions! But Izzy sat up a bit straighter. Jesus knew what it was like to feel sad?

He was sad because his friend had gone. His friend was called Lazarus and he'd died. But here's the thing, Izzy. Jesus knew that Lazarus would come back to life, because Jesus was going to make him alive again, but Jesus was still sad he was gone.

I know this is only a little letter, but I wanted to tell you about Jesus and being sad.

Love from Gran

Izzy read the letter again, then folded it carefully and put it back in Teddy's pocket with the others.

Jesus had missed his friend, even though he knew he'd see him again. A bit like Izzy with Mum. So Jesus really did know how she felt.

Had Gran done that on purpose? Izzy knew she couldn't have done, but it was strange that the letter was so relevant. Or *pertinent*, as the French would say. Izzy learned that word last week. It meant something connected with what was happening. Like the letter connected with Izzy feeling sad. It was really weird, though; there was no way Gran could have known Izzy would be upset right then. Actually, all the letters were helping, weren't they? But how come, if Gran didn't know? Izzy frowned, then smiled through her tears. Jesus! Of course, it was him! Not so long ago, Izzy didn't really think about Jesus, and when she had, it was just as someone in a Christmas play. He wasn't relevant to her life. But now, things were different. Izzy knew it was not only the letters that were pertinent and connected with her life. Jesus was *pertinent*, too.

Izzy jumped off the bed, grabbed her bag and dashed into the kitchen. She wasn't feeling so sad now, but she was running late! Snatching a slice of toast, Izzy waved goodbye to Aunty Elizabeth, and hurried out of the door.

'Bye!' said Aunty Elizabeth to the empty kitchen. 'Have a good day! See you later!' She finished off her coffee and then she, too, left the flat.

Izzy didn't like days when maths was her first lesson. It got the day off to a bad start, but today she was almost looking forward to it. She'd had fun doing maths with Aunty Elizabeth. Izzy's teacher would get a surprise! But when she arrived at the classroom, there was a cover teacher. Usually, Izzy would have been pleased, but this time, she felt a bit disappointed. Mrs McDonald was away. Izzy would have to wait until next week to surprise her.

After maths, it was science. Izzy was in the same class as Katy for science. As she walked along the corridor to Mr Simon's room, her heart began to beat a bit quicker, and she remembered the story of Zacchaeus. Maybe this would be a good time to get to know Katy. *Jesus, please help.*

When everyone was taking off their coats, and putting their bags down and finding seats, Katy went and sat by herself at a table in the corner. *Did she always do that?* Izzy frowned, as she sat at a table with her friends. *Did Katy always sit **alone**?* The others chatted about music and sport and hairstyles as they waited for Mr Simon to come, but Izzy was only half-listening. She was watching Katy. Katy had her hair covering her face, and her head was bent over the desk.

Mr Simon arrived, and everyone stopped talking. They stopped, and Mr Simon started. He talked about leaves, but he didn't talk about little lives inside the leaves. Izzy smiled to herself. Maybe no one else knew! *No one?* Well, no, of course no . . . Oh yes. Jesus knew! Zacchaeus was hidden inside leaves, yet Jesus knew he was there. Izzy glanced at Katy. Her hair was a bit like leaves, hiding her, but Jesus had shown Izzy that there was more to Katy than a head of hair. Now Izzy just needed to find her.

When it came to working in pairs, Kelly went with Jo.

Izzy knew she should be glad Kelly had friends, and she was glad. She really was. She liked having Kelly as a friend. But she sometimes didn't feel glad, like now, when she could see Jo and Kelly talking and laughing. Izzy was mixed up inside. She didn't know what to call how she felt. She knew she'd decided not to work with the gang, but Jo was her best friend. Not Kelly's. Just then, Jo looked up and pulled a face at Izzy. Izzy laughed. Jo hated science!

Izzy walked over to Katy.

'Can I work with you?'

Katy shrugged, a mixture of surprise and 'do what you want', but moved her bag so Izzy could sit down.

The room began to buzz with conversation. Izzy and Katy sat in silence. It was **AWKWARD**, and Izzy felt her cheeks turn red. Maybe she should have stayed with her friends, and worked with one of them. Why was she the one that had to work with Katy, anyway? Why didn't Jesus ask someone else? Izzy might as well be sitting on her own. It was too hard, trying to be with Katy, who didn't speak. *It's not too hard. We can do it together.* Jesus was with her. She wasn't on her own. He would help. If anyone knew about getting to know people and noticing them, it was Jesus. He was the one who noticed Zacchaeus up a tree! Izzy wished she was climbing trees; not because she liked climbing trees, but it would be easier than sitting here with Katy.

Izzy looked around the classroom. Everyone else had their heads bent over their work, close and talking to each other. Izzy and Katy were sitting apart.

'Jesus, **HELP**,' whispered Izzy inside. She moved her chair closer to Katy's.

Now what?

Izzy sighed. She couldn't think of anything clever or helpful to say.

'We'd better get on with this.'

Katy nodded, but she didn't start working. Instead, she drew little circles on her book. Izzy watched the pen, round and round. It was pressing so hard it nearly went through the paper.

Eventually, Katy spoke: 'Why?'

'Because Mr Simon said we have to.'

Katy glanced at Izzy through her hair, then looked back at the desk.

'No, I mean why did you come and sit with me?'

Izzy had never asked anyone that question. She felt bad that Katy was not used to having people sit with her.

'You've been off school for a while.'

Katy half-lifted her head.

'You mean you **noticed** I wasn't here?'

No one ever noticed Katy.

'Yes,' said Izzy, although she didn't say she'd only noticed last night.

'I was sick, that's why I didn't come to school.'

'You were sick every day?'

'No.' Katy's voice dropped to a whisper. 'Some days, I pretended.'

Katy had her head down, and her hair hid her face, but Izzy heard.

'You pretended to be sick?'

Katy stared at the desk.

'Why?'

Katy bit her lip. 'Because when I'm not at school, I don't have to be looked at.'

Izzy didn't know what to say. It was no use saying that of course people at school looked at her, Katy wasn't invisible, because Izzy knew why Katy said that. Or she could have a good guess.

Izzy waited for Katy to say more, but she didn't. After a while of silence, Izzy said, 'Right, we'd better do this work, but will you meet me at lunchtime?'

Katy turned to check Izzy wasn't joking. It would be great not to eat lunch alone for once! But did she dare? As she turned, out of the corner of her eye she saw Izzy's gang, sitting across the classroom.

Of course. Izzy had lots of friends. Katy had been silly to imagine, even for a second, that she could be brave enough. The whole crowd would be there, and Katy spent her life *HIDING* from crowds.

'No, it's OK.' She looked at the desk again.

Izzy saw where Katy had been looking.

'Please? It'll be just us. I think my other friends are busy this lunchtime, anyway.'

Izzy didn't add that they'd be 'busy' talking about boys, or hair, or make-up and messing around.

Slowly, Katy nodded. 'OK.'

Izzy had said 'my other friends'. Did that mean Izzy wanted Katy as a friend? No one ever did, but Izzy seemed different.

Izzy smiled. 'Great! Now, let's work on this . . . '

Katy was glad they were not talking about her anymore.

The two of them got on with their work until Mr Simon clapped his hands and, when everyone was quiet, said each group would tell the class about what they'd learned.

They all groaned.

Amber went to the front to report for her group, and Izzy hissed to Katy, 'I'll do our report.' Katy seemed **relieved** that she wouldn't have to stand at the front of the class. 'Thanks,' she whispered back.

Izzy went to the front to tell the class what she and Katy had learned about leaves, and reminded herself not to talk about leaf windows, and lives inside the leaves! She'd feel really silly if she did that!

After she'd given their report, the bell rang for end of lesson.

'You were great!' said Katy, as they gathered up their books.

'Thanks! See you at lunch? Meet you by the old tree.'

Katy watched Izzy walk over to her friends. The 'old tree' was behind the science block. No one ever really went there, and Katy knew that's why Izzy had suggested it.

As Katy walked out of the classroom, her hair still hid her face, but her face had a smile on.

During the next lesson, though, and the one before lunch, Katy began to wonder. Had Izzy really meant it? What if she just wanted to have a laugh when Katy waited all alone by the tree? Maybe it would be better not to go.

Katy had been so looking forward to lunchtime, but now she was dreading it. What if Izzy didn't turn up?

Lunchtime came, and Katy decided to just walk *past* the tree. That way, if Izzy was there, she could stop, but if she wasn't, she could just carry on walking, and no one would know.

Katy turned the corner of the science block.

There was the tree.

She casually glanced over at it.

Izzy was there! And she was alone.

She saw Katy coming, and waved. Katy **smiled** again. It hadn't been a wind-up.

Katy

Katy shrugged her rucksack off her back and sat down beside Izzy, leaning against the trunk of the tree.

'I'm glad we got that science project out of the way.' Izzy munched her cheese sandwich.

'Me too! Thanks for reporting back on ours, you were great.'

'That's OK. I don't mind doing that stuff, but I sometimes wish I could watch myself! I'd love to know how I look when I do it.'

'Would you? Really?'

'Yeah. I mean, it would probably be embarrassing, but I reckon it would be funny, too.'

Katy put down her half-eaten sandwich. She held her head up, flicked her hair behind her shoulders, and took a deep breath:

'OK, so, um, yeah, our project was, um, well, it was really interesting. Um . . .' Katy wound her long hair round the thumb of her left hand.

Izzy BURST out laughing.

'That's me, isn't it?'

Katy stopped. She pulled her hair down again and carried on eating her lunch.

'Sorry,' she mumbled.

'Why are you sorry? It was great!'

Katy lifted her eyes to Izzy. 'Really? You don't mind?'

'Why would I mind? It was brilliant!'

Katy was embarrassed, but in a good way.

'Thank you. I like mimicking!'

'I can't wait to tell my friends about this. They'll love it. Will you do them, too?'

Katy looked at the ground. An ant was crawling along. For a minute, she'd forgotten. She'd forgotten that she should be hiding, not having fun with other people.

'I can't,' she said, in a wobbly voice.

Izzy didn't say anything for a while.

'Katy? You know what you said earlier, about liking being away from school so that no one sees you?'

Katy **FROZE**.

'What did you mean when you said that?'

There was a long silence.

'Jhvlyfufutjf,' came from behind Katy's hair, which was now completely hiding her face as she rested her forehead on her bent knees.

'What?'

'Because of my face.'

'Because of your f . . . ?'

Izzy stopped. Katy had a big mark on her face. People said it was a burn mark. It went all the way from her forehead, and covered one cheek and some of her neck.

Izzy knew Katy got bullied for it. 'Strawberry!' 'Tomato Ketchup face!' 'Traffic light on stop!'

Izzy remembered her mum's red nail polish, pushing the doorbell at Aunty Elizabeth's, then shook the thought away.

No wonder Katy didn't like coming to school. Izzy wouldn't like it if she got bullied all the time.

'To be honest, I don't really notice your face.'

'Yeah right,' muttered Katy.

'It's true. Of course I see it, I'm not going to lie. But it's not the main thing about you.'

'Easy for you to say. You don't see it every time you look in a mirror.'

Katy was right. Izzy didn't see it in the mirror.

Jesus, help, please.

Izzy thought about the story in Gran's letter about Zacchaeus. All everyone noticed about Zacchaeus was how mean he was, and how he stole from them. But Jesus didn't even mention that part of him. Jesus looked **past** it to the person Zacchaeus was. A bit like Izzy with Katy. Izzy looked past Katy's burn mark.

Izzy tried to remember. What was it the letter had said? She pictured Teddy, lying on her bed at Aunty Elizabeth's. If only she'd brought the letter with her. Izzy closed her eyes. What had Jesus done? What had he said about the stealing, which was all people noticed?

Izzy couldn't remember. All she could remember was that Jesus walked along, said to Zacchaeus 'Come on, let's go', and then they went to Zacchaeus's house.

That was it! Jesus didn't say anything about Zacchaeus at all, he just said, 'Let's go.'

Izzy didn't need to say anything about Katy's face.

'Shall we go and find my friends? They can see you being me!'

'But . . . '

'We don't have to. We can just stay here if you want. But I think it would be fun.'

Izzy waited for Katy to decide and, at last, Katy nodded. OK. She was used to people laughing and staring at her face and so, if Izzy's friends did the same, Katy could just walk away. But it had been good with Izzy, and Katy wondered if she herself could be someone who had a group of friends. Not really, she knew that, but maybe for the rest of lunchtime she could pretend.

As they walked to where Izzy knew her friends would be, Izzy linked her arm through Katy's.

Jesus, please let them be nice. Then Izzy felt bad; of course her friends were nice!

'Hi, everyone,' she said, throwing her bag on the ground and sitting down, **pulling** Katy down beside her. The gang were sitting cross-legged in a circle and were surprised when they saw Katy. But they moved over to make space.

'Here's a puzzle for you,' Izzy carried on. 'How can I see myself without using a mirror, reflection, or camera?'

'What? What are you on about? You can't!' Jo looked at the others. They didn't know either.

'Oh, really?' Izzy gave Katy a nudge and a whispered, 'Go on.'

Katy swallowed nervously. Everyone was looking at her. She hated it when people looked at her.

Taking a deep breath, she held her head up, flicked her hair back, and started mimicking people. She did Izzy, then she did the king, then she did a girl from Year 11, then she did an actress.

When she'd finished, no one said anything. They just stared at her. Jo's mouth was slightly open.

Katy wanted to get away. She should have known it was too good to be true. Why did she ever think she'd fit in with a group? Head down, hair hiding her face, she began to put her bag on her shoulder and stand up, when she heard a clap. Then another joining in. Soon, the whole gang were clapping. For her!

'That was AMAZING!' said Kelly.

'Where did you learn to do that?' asked Jo.

'Can you mimic a teacher?' That was Lucy.

There were all talking at once.

'Um.' Katy wasn't sure where to begin, and everyone started laughing. Katy laughed, too. It was funny, all of them talking at once!

They repeated what they'd said, one at a time.

'Thank you, Kelly.' Katy felt shy. Never in a million years would she have thought someone at school would tell her she'd done something amazing. Not without being sarcastic, anyway. And now two had! First Izzy, then Kelly. And all the others clapped, too.

She turned to Jo. 'I didn't learn, it's just something I've always done. It's like when I watch people, I see the way they are, and I just want to mimic them.'

'Wow.' Jo was impressed. 'You're really good at it.'

Katy came to Lucy's question. Could she do a teacher?

She sat up straight and clapped her hands. She stretched her neck long and held her head to one side, wagging her finger.

'It's Mrs Walker,' they all squealed, rolling around with laughter.

Katy had to stop because she was **giggling** so much.

'Did you hear about what happened in PE?' asked Lucy 'You'll never believe it . . .'

The conversation moved on, Katy joining in. For the first time in a long time, she had forgotten about hiding her face, and she was having fun.

The bell rang, and the girls stood up, collecting their bags and coats.

'Have you got French next?' Kelly asked. Katy nodded. 'Me too.'

The gang went separate ways. 'See you later!'

'See you later, Katy,' called Lucy. 'See you later!' Katy called back. Katy walked beside Kelly, thinking that this was one of the best days ever.

After school, as Izzy walked towards the gate, she saw Kelly and Katy together. She laughed at herself. Why had she ever thought her friends wouldn't be nice?

At the gate, she couldn't help looking to see if Aunty Elizabeth's car was there. It wasn't, but Amy's aunty was there waiting to pick Amy up.

Never mind, Izzy told herself. *It doesn't matter.* But as she walked up the road, she knew it did matter to her really. She KICKED a stone along the pavement. Was it too much to ask, to have an aunty who actually noticed her? She kicked the stone harder, feeling more and more sorry for herself, and she forgot about the maths help and the pizza. She was the only one who had an aunty who didn't care. She kicked the stone so hard it bounced then fell down a drain.

Izzy got to the flat before Aunty Elizabeth. She let herself in, took her shoes off and went to her bedroom, stopping on the way to get a drink. *That's the drink Aunty Elizabeth bought for you because you don't like coffee.* 'Oh, great.' But Izzy supposed Jesus was right. She knew he was reminding her that Aunty Elizabeth did notice her. She still wished she'd meet her after school, though.

Teddy was lying on her bed, and the little pocket on his jeans seemed to be calling: 'Izzy!' She knew there was another letter waiting and she was tempted to open it now, but she told herself to wait.

Beginning to do her homework, Izzy struggled to concentrate. She was not so angry at Aunty Elizabeth, but now she couldn't stop thinking about Katy. Did Katy remember getting burned? It must have been so scary. Katy hated her face. Izzy wished there was something she could do to help. *Tomorrow*, she decided, *I will try to talk with Katy. I don't know what I'll say. At least Jesus will be with me.*

Izzy turned back to her books.

She was reading about cloud formations when she heard the front door **slam**.

'I'm home!' called Aunty Elizabeth.

Aunty Elizabeth stopped still. She hadn't intended to call out, but it felt surprisingly good. Was it really less than a week since she'd stood in the very place she was standing now, by the front door, waiting for the doorbell to ring? She'd wanted to put her fingers in her ears and not open the door. What did she know about having 11-year-old girls to stay? Especially ones she'd never met. And this wasn't just any girl, it was her niece, her sister's daughter.

As she thought about her sister, she realized she felt a bit less angry than she usually did where Sally was concerned.

'Hi! I'll be out in a minute!' came floating from Izzy's bedroom. When had she started thinking of the spare room as Izzy's bedroom? Things were changing.

Together

Aunty Elizabeth was in the kitchen, making herself a coffee, when Izzy appeared. Izzy poured herself some juice.

'How's Suzy?' Aunty Elizabeth asked, as they sat down with their drinks.

Izzy hadn't seen Suzy properly all day. She'd passed her in the corridor, though, and invited her round tomorrow.

'She says she'd love to come tomorrow.'

'Good. We'll have to think about what to give her to eat.'

'Mmm.' Izzy was only half-listening. Suzy had stopped and talked to her in the corridor, without being mean or acting cool. Suzy had even given her a quick hug before they dashed to their next lessons. Things were fine with Suzy, and Izzy was looking forward to tomorrow.

'I didn't see Suzy much today, but I saw Katy.'

'Katy? You've not mentioned her before. You have a lot of friends!'

'Katy is not really my friend. Well, she wasn't before today.'

Izzy **chewed** her lip.

'What's the matter?'

'Katy has a burn on her face and she hates it, and I told her I don't really notice it, and she said "yeah right", and she didn't believe me, but it's true.'

Izzy brushed tears from her eyes.

'I want to talk to her again tomorrow, but I don't know what to say.'

Jesus will help me, but Izzy didn't say that bit out loud.

Aunty Elizabeth came and gave Izzy a **hug**.

Pulling back, she kept her hands on her niece's shoulders. 'Izzy? Would you like to . . .? I mean, we could . . .' Aunty Elizabeth shook her head. 'It doesn't matter. We don't have to.'

'Don't have to what?'

'I just thought we could maybe, um, talk to Jesus about it? You know, ask him to help you tomorrow? But it's fine, don't worry about it.'

Aunty Elizabeth reached to pick up their empty cups.

Izzy put out a hand to stop her.

'Really? Did you mean it?'

Aunty Elizabeth sat down again. Had she meant it? It was so hard seeing Izzy upset, and this was the only thing she could think of to help. Talking to Jesus at breakfast had reminded her of a long time ago. A time she'd forgotten about.

'When I was your age, Izzy, I used to go every week to a church youth group. I went with my friend. She believed all that stuff about Jesus, and she went to church as well, but to be honest I really only went because a boy I liked went.'

'Did he like you, too?' asked Izzy. It was hard to imagine Aunty Elizabeth being her age.

'No, in the end he went out with my friend instead. All my efforts were for nothing!'

Izzy **sniggered**. Talking about boys with Aunty Elizabeth felt a bit weird.

Aunty Elizabeth carried on. 'At the end of each youth group session we all sat together, and someone talked about God, or the Bible. I only half-listened. But just before they finished, they always asked if anyone had anything they wanted prayer for. I learned that meant talk to Jesus about stuff. So people would talk to Jesus about their grandad in hospital, or their brilliant exam results. Anything, really. I never said anything but I always liked that bit, and you've reminded me of it. I never talked to Jesus in this flat until you came!'

Izzy wished she could have gone to that youth group. She wanted to talk to Jesus about tomorrow with Aunty Elizabeth, but she didn't know how. If she went to that youth group, maybe she'd know. She knew what it was like to talk to Jesus just her, but what was it like to talk to him with someone else?

Just like when you say grace together. She knew that was Jesus!

'OK,' said Izzy, suddenly shy. 'Let's talk to Jesus about it. But what do we have to do? Do we need to kneel, or go somewhere?'

'I don't think so,' Aunty Elizabeth's forehead creased as she remembered how they all used to pray while they lolled around on beanbags at youth group. 'Right here will be fine.'

'OK.' Izzy put her elbows on the table, and rested her chin on her hands. 'Jesus, I'm really worried about tomorrow. Please help me be a good friend to Katy, just like you were to Zacchaeus. Amen.'

'Amen,' said Aunty Elizabeth. 'And Jesus, **thank you** for Izzy.' Izzy looked up in surprise, but Aunty Elizabeth carried on, 'Thank you that she is so thoughtful. Help her know what to say to Katy tomorrow. Amen.'

'Amen.'

It felt good to talk to Jesus together and, as Izzy looked at her aunt, she could tell it had felt good to Aunty Elizabeth, too.

'Right,' said Aunty Elizabeth. 'I'm just going to have a shower, and then I'll make a start on dinner.'

Izzy nodded, absently. She was thinking about lives in leaves. Did they have youth group?

Later, over dinner, Aunty Elizabeth asked, 'Who's Zacchaeus?'

What? Oh yeah, Izzy had mentioned Zacchaeus when she prayed. She'd forgotten that Aunty Elizabeth didn't know about the letters! Izzy wasn't ready to share her secret yet.

'Someone who was Jesus' friend.'

'Zacchaeus,' said Aunty Elizabeth, thoughtfully. 'It's an interesting name. Why don't we Google it after dinner?'

They finished eating, washed up, and Aunty Elizabeth pulled out her laptop.

'Come and sit with me,' she said, and Izzy sat and watched Aunty Elizabeth type in Zakeus. That wasn't how Gran spelled it in the letter! Izzy was right, but Google gave the option 'Zacchaeus'. 'Click on that one,' Izzy pointed.

Izzy leaned across and, heads bent close together, they looked at the screen. It said the story about Zacchaeus was a story from the bible. Were all the stories in Gran's letters from the Bible?

After they'd finished reading, Aunty Elizabeth sat back. 'Zacchaeus wasn't very nice, was he? Stealing from people like that. Don't you think it's strange that Jesus still wanted to be his friend? Why would he? When someone was mean to me, I didn't want to be their friend anymore.'

Izzy looked at Aunty Elizabeth and wondered who she was talking about. Someone had been mean to her?

'Maybe you could try to be their friend again? That's what Jesus would do, isn't it?'

'Yes, but Jesus didn't have to deal with your m – ' Aunty Elizabeth stopped too late. Izzy could fill in the blank. Your mum. Izzy felt **DEFENSIVE** towards her mum. Why wouldn't Aunty Elizabeth even say her name? What had happened with those two? Izzy opened her mouth to ask, saw the look on Aunty Elizabeth's face, then shut it again.

'I think I'll go to bed now.' What she really meant was, I'll go and read my next letter from Gran!

'OK, sleep well,' replied Aunty Elizabeth. Izzy wondered if she was still thinking about Jesus and Zacchaeus.

Izzy hesitated, then gave Aunty Elizabeth a quick hug, before turning and going straight to her bedroom. She didn't see the little smile on Aunty Elizabeth's face as she watched her niece close the door behind her.

Izzy flopped onto her bed and stared at the ceiling. She couldn't stop a smile crossing her face. Had she really prayed with Aunty Elizabeth, and read a story from the Bible? Even with the issue with her mum, whatever it was, it had been a good evening.

She looked out of the window and, in the fading light, she could just make out the leaf windows. She hoped the people behind them were having a good evening, too.

Izzy raised herself onto an elbow, unzipped Teddy's pocket and took out the next letter from Gran. What would this one say? Would it be from the Bible, too?

The first letter had been about getting to know Jesus. Izzy was getting to know him, and she was getting to know Aunty Elizabeth, too. Maybe the story about Jesus being born was in the Bible?

The second letter had been about giving what we can to help others. Izzy thought back to Kelly and the grass buzz. Now Kelly was a good friend. And now Izzy knew that maybe the story about the boy and his picnic was in the Bible.

The third letter had been about noticing people. Izzy had noticed Suzy, and she'd learned that there was more to Aunty Elizabeth than it seemed. The story about the woman going into the crowd to see Jesus might be in the Bible, too!

Last night's letter had been about being a friend. Izzy thought about Katy. They'd had a brilliant time together. Izzy giggled as she remembered Katy mimicking her. She'd forgotten to tell Aunty Elizabeth about that. It had been so funny! Katy was part of the gang now. The only thing was, Katy didn't believe Izzy about her face. Tomorrow Izzy was going to try to talk to her about it. 'No idea how I'm going to do that,' she muttered to herself. She opened an envelope and smoothed out today's letter.

Dear Izzy

Today Helen and I went shopping. We went to the shop we always go to, you know, the one with Mrs Smith who used to give you sweets when you were little? I know, I know, you're not little anymore; but I notice you don't mind that she still gives you sweets!

Izzy smiled. That was true.

When we got to the counter to buy our shopping, Mrs Smith looked really upset. She said she'd just had some boys in the shop from the boys' high school. She doesn't mind them going in, but today there was a younger boy already in the shop. He was wearing the same school uniform, and the big lads started picking on him. They grabbed his bag and put it in the freezer with the peas.

Izzy giggled, then stopped herself. She felt sorry for the boy, but it was funny about the peas!

They opened a can of coke and poured it over his head.

Izzy wasn't giggling now.

They called him squinty four eyes because he wears glasses.

They made fun of his shoes.

Mrs Smith kept trying to help, but they just pushed her away. In the end she said she would call the police if they didn't get out of her shop. She's never going to let them back in, either. They are banned.

As we walked home, Helen told me it reminded her of a story from the Bible. She said all the Jesus stories are from the Bible.

Izzy thought about Googling 'Zakeus' with Aunty Elizabeth, and reading from the Bible together on the screen. So they are all from the Bible. *Yes, Gran, I worked that out!* Izzy wished she could really tell Gran.

This next story is from the first bit of the Bible, which mainly uses the name 'God' rather than 'Jesus'. Helen told me that, so I am telling you! The story is about someone called Samuel. God – remember Jesus is the Son of God – told Samuel to go and choose a king, and he said the king would be one of a man called Jesse's sons. So Samuel went, and all the sons lined up. The first son was tall, good-looking, strong – I think he would have looked like one of those pop stars you like.

That made Izzy laugh.

But God told Samuel not to choose that one. The others were all good-looking too, but God said don't choose them either. There was one more brother, but he was just a boy. They fetched him anyway, and God told Samuel that was the one he'd chosen.

Helen said that God said – oh what was it – that's right: people look at how things look on the outside, but God looks inside people, to their hearts. He sees how they think and feel.

I wish those boys had tried to look in the way God looks, and seen who the boy was inside. Mrs Smith said the boy was really nice, they talked while she helped him dry his hair and get his bag out of the freezer.

Love from Gran

Izzy folded the letter, put it back in its envelope and slipped it into Teddy's pocket. She cleaned her teeth and climbed into bed. Gran's letter said God thought **inside** was more important than outside. Aunty Elizabeth had said the same about Suzy, too. Maybe Izzy could tell Katy tomorrow. Inside is more important.

Izzy wasn't sure how she felt about Jesus seeing how she was on the inside, because it meant that Jesus could see the not-so-good things, too. Izzy knew she wasn't perfect, she knew she got cross and said the wrong thing, and wasn't always very nice. But it was one thing her knowing it, and quite another to think that Jesus knew it.

She grabbed Teddy and began looking through his pocket. She wanted to get the very first letter out again. There it was. She pulled the letter from its little envelope, and scanned the words. Her finger pointed at the bit she'd been looking for: 'Jesus knows everything'. So, right from the start of becoming Jesus' friend, he'd known all about her. He'd known all along that she wasn't perfect, and he still helped her and stayed with her. He still wanted to be her friend. That was alright, then. Izzy put the letter back in Teddy's pocket, and lay down in bed.

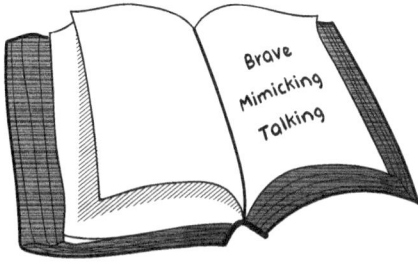

Flipping onto her stomach, she picked up her Word Book. What words today?

Brave. She had felt brave when she'd gone to sit with Katy.

Mimicking. Obviously!

Talking. She'd talked with Katy and Aunty Elizabeth and Jesus. She'd talked to Jesus with Aunty Elizabeth, too. Yes, 'talking' was a good word today.

Izzy wrote Brave, Mimicking, Talking, then put the Word Book back on the floor by her bed.

As she lay back down, she thought about meeting Katy under the tree. Izzy hadn't realized it before, but the tree was a great place to meet, and not just because it was a place where no one went. Zacchaeus and Jesus had met under a tree. Izzy and Katy had done the same, though neither of them had climbed the tree first! There was the leaves link, too. Izzy imagined lives going on unseen inside leaves, but Katy really did have a life where she wasn't seen. So did Zacchaeus.

Izzy leaned over and switched off the light.

Thursday

'Jesus, thank you for our breakfast,' said Aunty Elizabeth the next morning, as they sat at the breakfast table.

'Amen,' mumbled Izzy, picking up her spoon to eat her cornflakes. She was feeling **GRUMPY**. Talking to Katy had seemed like a good idea, but now the day was here, Izzy wasn't so sure.

But Aunty Elizabeth hadn't finished.

'. . . please help Izzy today. Help her know what to say. Amen.'

Aunty Elizabeth remembered! And she'd talked to Jesus about it.

As Izzy walked to school, she was wondering how she'd get Katy on her own.

First lesson was science, but when Mr Simon told the class to work in pairs, Kelly went with Katy.

Second lesson was history, but Katy and Izzy were not in the same class for that.

All morning, every time Izzy thought she might have a chance to talk to Katy, it didn't happen.

Jesus, what's going on? I thought you wanted me to talk to Katy?

Jesus?

Hello?

Izzy didn't know what to do. She'd become used to having Jesus with her, and talking to her, and now she felt alone. Had Jesus decided not to be her friend?

A game she sometimes used to play with her friends called 'Knowledge is Power' came into her mind. It was a game where you had to choose the right answer from a list before you could move up a level. It was all about what you knew.

Where had that thought come from? She hadn't played that game for ages.

Jesus. Of course. Trust him to remind her through a video game! She knew Jesus was there, and listening to her. She knew he was her friend. She knew it was true.

Knowledge is Power.

Izzy caught up with Kelly and Katy as they walked over to the gang's lunchtime place.

Suddenly, Kelly stopped. 'I've left my bag in the woodwork room! It's got my lunch in it. I'll go and get it. Meet you with the others.'

Izzy was puzzled. Kelly was one of the most organized people she knew! It was so unlike her to forget her bag. But now just Katy and Izzy were left. *This is what I've been waiting for*, thought Izzy, *so why do I feel so nervous?*

Izzy linked her arm through Katy's and walked in the direction of the tree where they'd sat yesterday.

Jesus. **help!** *What do I do now?*

Just be honest.

She was glad he'd answered. But just be honest? What did that mean? Just tell Katy straight?

Maybe Izzy had been making this too complicated.

They sat down under the tree, and Izzy said, 'I've been thinking about what you said yesterday.'

'Which bit?'

'About your face.'

'Oh.' Katy put her sandwich down, automatically putting up her hand to cover her face.

'What happened?'

Katy closed her eyes. Echoes of voices from the past filled her head, faster and faster, round and round: 'What's happened to your face?', 'What's happened to your face?'

No one really wanted to know, they were just laughing at her. And now Izzy was doing the same.

But when Katy opened her eyes, she saw that Izzy was just sitting, waiting. Did she really want to know what happened? Perhaps she did.

'It happened when I was 6.' Katy began to cry.

Izzy didn't know what to do, so she didn't do anything.

Taking a deep breath, Katy started talking, her voice coming fast and jerky. 'It was on Christmas Day, when I was 6. The Christmas tree caught fire when we'd all gone to bed, and the fire started burning the whole house. I can remember waking up and my eyes were stinging, and I was coughing and I couldn't breathe. I shouted "Mummy" but my voice would only whisper. My bedroom door was open, and smoke was coming through it. I got out of bed and went across to the door. I was coughing and I was hot. When I was nearly at the door, I saw the flames. Suddenly there was a **BANG**, and I fell over, and that's the last thing I remember about the fire. When I woke up, I was in hospital. My head was in a bandage, with holes for my eyes and mouth.'

Katy hadn't finished yet.

'Afterwards I was told that the explosion blew part of the banister off the wall. It was burning and flew through the air, and landed on my face when I was lying on the ground. The firefighters who rescued me were amazed more of me didn't burn.'

Katy's voice dropped. 'Sometimes I wish so much of me burned that I died.'

Izzy was shocked. Katy wished she was dead?

'I'm glad you're not dead.'

Katy started crying again.

'If you were dead, who would make me laugh by mimicking?'

Katy managed a **smile** through her tears. She turned to look at Izzy.

'Izzy? Did you mean what you said yesterday? About not really noticing my face? Tell me the truth.'

Izzy looked at her friend. She knew she needed to be honest, she owed it to Katy.

'I did notice it at first, and I wondered what happened. But then I didn't really think about it or you. Sorry, but you told me to be honest! Now, I do still notice your face, I guess, but not in a bad way or anything. It's just part of you, like I notice Emma's glasses, or Anna's freckles.'

'So my face doesn't matter to you?'

'Like I said, it's not the main thing about you.'

Katy was quiet.

'Why did you come and sit with me in science?'

Izzy didn't know what to say. The question took her by surprise. Maybe she could just say because she'd wanted to? But that wasn't the whole story, and Katy had asked her to be honest. Jesus had suggested being honest, too.

'Because you were on your own, and I thought you might like it if someone sat with you.'

'But Izzy, I'm always on my own. Whenever I come to school, I'm on my own. I always have been, you know that. So why?'

Izzy thought about it. The honest answer was 'because of my friend Jesus', but she'd never talked about him with anyone. Well, a bit with Aunty Elizabeth, but that was all.

Katy was waiting.

Izzy tried to sound **CASUAL**.

'Katy, do you believe in Jesus?'

Now it was Katy's turn to be surprised!

'Well, I don't not believe in him. I never really think about God now. Why did you ask that?'

'Because,' said Izzy, shyly, 'the honest answer to your question about why I sat with you yesterday is because of Jesus.'

Izzy wasn't ready to tell anyone about Teddy and the letters.

'There are stories about him in the Bible, and he seems really nice and always noticed people. I thought that was a good way to be.'

'Do you think Jesus would even notice people like me, though?' Katy touched her face.

Izzy thought so. Jesus had noticed her when she was happy, sad, grumpy. He always noticed her. He wouldn't let scars stop him noticing anyone.

She hugged Katy.

'definitely.'

Katy smiled a real smile.

'It's funny you asked about God. When I first came to this school, I started going to CU.'

Izzy took a bite of her sandwich.

'What's CU?' she asked as she chewed. 'I've seen it on the timetable, but I don't know what it is.'

'CU stands for Christian Union, and people go there and hang out and talk about Jesus, and how he helps them.'

Izzy nodded. That made sense. Jesus helped her.

'Don't you go anymore?'

Katy picked up a leaf and twirled it in her hand.

'I stopped going. People talked about how much Jesus loves us and wants to be our friend, and that was good, but then one week, where I was sitting meant I could see my reflection in the window.'

Izzy could guess what was coming.

'I thought, why would Jesus love me, and want me to be his friend? Look at me. No one wants to be my friend. I picked up my bag, and walked out of the room, and I never went back.'

They sat in silence for a while, then Izzy asked, 'Is CU on at lunchtimes?'

'Yes, every Friday.'

'That's tomorrow! I'd like to go. At least I think I would, but . . .'

'But what?'

Izzy looked at the sky. 'I'm a bit nervous about going.'

'You're nervous? You're never nervous!'

Izzy laughed. 'I am! People are **more** than what we see on the outside.'

Now it was Katy's turn to put an arm round Izzy's shoulders and give her a hug. She knew Izzy had said that on purpose. Katy wanted to help her friend.

'Would it help if I came to CU with you?'

'Seriously? It would help loads! But I thought you don't go now?'

Katy took a deep breath.

'It's OK. I'd like to go. If you can notice me and be my friend, maybe Jesus can too. Maybe I should give him a chance.'

Izzy smiled. This was the first time she'd really talked about Jesus with anyone apart from Aunty Elizabeth.

'OK, great, we'll both go to CU tomorrow. Come on, let's go and find the others.'

They stood up, brushing the grass from their skirts.

'Izzy, do you think the others mind about my face?'

Izzy linked her arm through Katy's, and they started walking. 'No. I think they're like me. They know that who you are is way more important than what you look like.'

Katy **RELAXED**. For the first time she could remember, she felt really happy. When they got near to their friends, it was Katy who waved. 'Hi, everyone!' Just then, a gust of wind blew her hair back, away from her face. She let her hair blow free. Inside was more important than how she looked.

See You There

'Where've you two been?' asked Kelly, as Izzy and Katy sat down beside the others.

The other girls joined in:

'We wondered where you'd got to!'

'Are you OK?'

'We're fine,' said Izzy.

'We were just talking,' Katy glanced at Izzy.

'And you know how much I can talk!' Everyone laughed when Izzy said that, and they forgot to ask what Izzy and Katy had talked about.

Katy was grateful. She wasn't ready to talk to more people about her face just yet. Once had been hard enough. She was glad she'd done it, though.

The bell rang, and they reluctantly stood up. Katy handed Kelly her crutches, and the girls headed off to their next lesson. Drama was the only class they all had together.

Everyone piled into the drama studio and found a place to sit on the floor. There were no desks in drama, which was great. They liked sitting on the floor.

Ms Berry looked around the group, and picked Katy to go to the front and read part of the play they were studying.

Katy's heart sank. She always dreaded having to go to the front of the class, with people looking at her. She glanced at her new friends, and they all smiled and gave her a **thumbs up**. Katy managed a small smile back, then pulled her hair to hide her face, and walked to the front of the class. When she got there, she turned around and saw everyone. Some were nudging each other and whispering. There were her friends at the back. They were still smiling and giving her a thumbs up. They saw more than her burn scars.

Katy opened her book at the right page. The class were still nudging and whispering, but Katy remembered her friends encouraging her. She held her head up, flicked back her hair, and began to read. Gradually, hers was the only voice in the classroom. The whispering stopped. They were all watching in stunned silence. Katy could act!

When Katy finished, there was quiet for a while. Then she heard a clap. It was Suzy. Katy pulled her hair to cover her face again. How could she have been stupid enough to think she could be accepted? Suzy was being sarcastic; Suzy always knew how to make people feel bad.

But then Katy heard another clap, and another joining in. Soon, everyone in the class was cLaPPinG – including Ms Berry. Katy was embarrassed, but in a good way. They were clapping because they thought she'd done a good job, not laughing at her because of her face. As Katy went to sit back down, she thought that maybe Izzy was right. Her face wasn't the most important thing about her. When she passed Suzy, she gave her a little smile. It was Suzy who had started off the clapping.

'That was brilliant,' the gang whispered to her as she sat down.

'Thanks!' Katy whispered back.

After school, they all went their separate ways.

'Bye! See you at our place tomorrow lunchtime!'

'OK!'

Then Izzy remembered about CU. 'Hang on a minute, come back!' she called, and the girls all came and stood in a group again. What did Izzy want?

'Um, tomorrow lunchtime Katy and I thought we'd go to CU.'

'To see who?' asked Jo.

'No, CU stands for Christian Union.' Izzy's heart beat fast as she said it, she knew the gang would think it was weird. At least Katy was there.

They all looked at Izzy, thinking she must be joking. No one knew what to say. Christian Union? Wasn't that the place where the Jesus kids went? Why would Izzy go there?!

Jo broke the awkward silence.

'CU could have a strapline: "See You There!"' She nudged Lucy. 'Get it? C U there!' and the two of them fell about laughing.

'Why not?'

They stopped laughing. 'Why not what, Izzy?'

'Why not "see you there"? Let's all go.'

The gang looked at each other. Go to Christian Union? With the *JESUS KIDS*?

'I don't think so,' said Lucy. 'Why would I want to do that?'

'Gary goes,' said Katy.

Izzy shot Katy a look. What had Gary got to do with it?

Gary had been born in Sweden, and moved to the UK when he was 5. He went to the boys' school round the corner from the girls' school, and the two schools sometimes got together for things like plays, or concerts. Izzy hadn't realized they got together for CU.

119

Izzy waited for Lucy to make a funny comment, but she just turned BRIGHT RED.

'I guess we can give CU a go.' Lucy tried to sound casual.

One by one, the others nodded. Why not give it a go? Izzy was their friend, and she wanted to go.

They said goodbye again, and went off, leaving Katy and Izzy standing there.

'How do you know Lucy likes Gary?' asked Izzy. 'I didn't know that.'

'When I was on my own a lot, I didn't say much, but I watched people. I saw that Lucy is always looking over at Gary if our schools get together.'

Was she? Izzy decided to watch them next time. Katy was probably right, especially as Lucy had turned red!

Just then, Suzy came up.

'Hi!'

Izzy could see Suzy's crowd staring. They couldn't believe Suzy would go off with Izzy and Katy after school.

'Hi, Suzy,' said Izzy. 'Let's go.'

The three of them began to walk towards the school gate. Katy was surprised Suzy had joined them, but she didn't say so.

'Suzy?'

'Yep?'

'I wanted to say thank you for, you know, in drama.'

'No problem, you were great!'

'Thanks.' Katy waved goodbye to the other two, and as she turned out of the gate for home, she was smiling. When she got home and Mum asked about her day, for the first time in a long time she'd be able to say it had been really good.

Izzy and Suzy walked in the opposite direction from Katy. Izzy looked for Aunty Elizabeth's car, but she didn't expect it to be there and it wasn't.

Bully

When Izzy and Suzy got to Aunty Elizabeth's flat, she wasn't home yet. Izzy let them in and made drinks, which the girls took into the sitting room. They then curled up at opposite ends of the sofa.

They talked a bit about school, and how great Katy was in drama, and how neither of them liked maths. 'How's things at home?' asked Izzy. 'You know, with Jack and your mum?'

'Do you know what? It's been a bit **better**. I still have to do things for Jack, but Mum has at least talked to me as well. Last night, we even played a game on my Xbox together. I was playing on my own and after Mum put Jack to bed, she came and asked if she could play, too. Normally she'd go and clear the kitchen up, or do something else, but she said that could wait. It was so funny playing the game with her! I tried to teach her what to do, but she couldn't do it; it was hilarious watching her try!'

Izzy giggled. *Thank you, Jesus.*

'Maybe you can come to my house and we'll play it,' said Suzy.

Suzy didn't usually ask friends to her house, not even her gang, because it was all about Jack.

'Yeah, OK, that would be great.'

'What about your mum?' Suzy asked. 'I mean, this is your aunt's flat, right?'

Izzy nodded. 'I miss my mum. She's away with my gran at the moment.'

Suzy was about to say something, when the girls heard a key in the lock. Aunty Elizabeth was home. Suzy gave Izzy a quick hug instead.

'We're in the sitting room!' called Izzy, and a few moments later, Aunty Elizabeth walked in.

'Hi, Izzy, and you must be Suzy? It's nice to meet you, welcome.'

'Thank you for having me.' Suzy felt embarrassed.

'It's lovely to have you. Let me just go and get changed, I won't be long.'

When Aunty Elizabeth returned, having swapped her work clothes for jeans and a jumper, she brought more drinks, and a bowl of chocolate buttons.

'Shall we play a game?'

Izzy breathed a sigh of relief. She'd been worried that Aunty Elizabeth would start asking Suzy questions.

Soon they were kneeling round the coffee table, playing UNO. They played a few rounds, and at the end, Aunty Elizabeth picked up a pen, pretending it was a microphone. Putting on an American accent, she announced:

'In third place, with a brilliant effort, we have . . . ' she tapped her hands in a DRUMROLL on the coffee table . . . 'Izzy!' She and Suzy clapped and cheered, and Izzy was presented with a chocolate button.

'In second place, showing that us old people can still play, we have . . .' drumroll . . . 'Me!' Izzy and Suzy clapped and cheered, and Izzy presented her aunt with two chocolate buttons.

'And now, the moment we've all been waiting for, in first place we have the amazing, the talented, Super Suzy!'

Izzy drummed her hands on the table and watched as Aunty Elizabeth presented Suzy with three chocolate buttons.

'Well done us!' said Aunty Elizabeth. 'Now, I'm just going to get dinner ready.' And she gathered up the empty cups, and went off to the kitchen.

'Your aunty is amazing!'

'Yeah, she's OK.' *She's more than OK. A lot has changed in a week!*

'Suzy? What do your friends think about you hanging out with me?'

'Um, I think they're a bit surprised.'

Izzy laughed. That was probably an understatement!

'But I like hanging out with you. I always wanted to, you know? I used to watch you and your crowd and wish I could join in. I had to keep being mean and tough, though. I am trying to be different, and – '

'Yes,' Izzy interrupted, 'like when you clapped for Katy in drama?'

'You noticed?'

'Yep. Shall we have another game of UNO?'

They'd nearly finished the game when they heard Aunty Elizabeth calling them for dinner.

'We'd better call it a draw,' Izzy stood up.

'OK. Even though I was winning!' teased Suzy.

Izzy nudged her, laughing.

As they sat down at the kitchen table, Izzy remembered about saying grace. Would they still say it with Suzy there? Izzy didn't know what to do. *Jesus! Help!*

'Suzy,' said Aunty Elizabeth. 'We normally say grace before we eat. Are you OK with that?'

Grace? Suzy never said grace. Well, except when she visited her grandparents – who were really old – and that was only about once a year. Suzy usually daydreamed through it. But Izzy's aunty was cool, and she said grace? Cool people did that?

'Yes, fine.'

'Great!'

'Jesus,

Thank you that Suzy is here, and thank you for our food.

Amen.'

'That's it?' blurted Suzy. 'I mean, "Amen", but that's it?'

'What do you mean?' Aunty Elizabeth began to eat her sausages.

Suzy thought of saying grace at her grandparents'.

'Don't you have to use special words and things?'

'I don't think so,' said Izzy. 'I don't use special words with you, and talking to Jesus is just like talking to a friend.'

'Oh.' Suzy had never thought of that before. Maybe she could try it. But Jesus? Suzy didn't even know if she believed in God and all that stuff. But she was pleased Aunty Elizabeth said 'Thank you that Suzy is here'. It made her feel wanted.

'How was your day, girls?' asked Aunty Elizabeth.

'Katy got a round of applause in drama, which was great cos usually people just bully her.'

As soon as the words were out of her mouth, Izzy wished she could take them back. Suzy had turned red, and Izzy knew she was thinking about times she'd been one of the bullies. Izzy kicked herself. Why hadn't she just kept her mouth shut?

Suzy looked at her plate. It was nice of Izzy not to say it, but she felt uncomfortable. She **SQUIRMED** on her seat. 'I'm one of those people.'

'Not today you weren't,' said Izzy. 'You're the one that started all the clapping!'

'Thanks,' Suzy smiled at her. 'I'm trying, but sometimes I just think I will always be a bully. It's how people expect me to be and, to be fair, it's how I normally am.'

Aunty Elizabeth took a sip of water.

'I used to be a bully.'

Suzy's forehead creased. 'You're just saying that, aren't you, to make me feel better?'

'No, it's true.'

'Oh.' Suzy couldn't imagine Izzy's aunty bullying people.

'Well, how did you STOP?'

'Like you, I knew it wouldn't be easy. But I didn't like being a bully, so I tried to stop. I did things like you did today, clapping when before you'd have made rude comments. It was hard and people didn't believe me at first, they still avoided me, but I kept refusing to be the bully they thought I was, and in the end they realized I meant it.'

'That's like Zacchaeus!' said Izzy.

'Who's Zacchaeus?' Suzy looked around to see if anyone was hiding in the kitchen.

Izzy laughed. 'He's not here, he's in a story we read in the Bible.'

'You guys read the Bible?'

'Well, we only have once,' Aunty Elizabeth smiled, 'so it might be a push to say we read it!'

Izzy thought about Teddy and the letters, where Gran told her things from the Bible. She'd read from the Bible more than once.

'So who's Z – whatever his name is?' Suzy laughed as she tried to pronounce his name.

'He's someone who was mean to people, and then he met Jesus and wanted to stop being mean. So he did, but it took people a while to believe he'd really changed, and wasn't tricking them.'

Suzy wasn't laughing now. She was listening. 'And did they? Did they believe him in the end?'

'Yes.'

Suzy tried to take it all in. Could she really stop being a bully? Would Jesus really help her? If he was even real.

'Suzy,' Aunty Elizabeth turned to her. 'Remind me to give your mum my number. If she's happy to let you have it, you can call me if you want – sometimes it helps to have someone who knows what it's like.'

'Thanks.' Suzy felt strange, but in a good way. She wasn't on her own anymore.

When they'd finished dinner, they washed up. Aunty Elizabeth put music on, and soon the three of them were dancing around the kitchen, flicking soap suds at each other. Who knew that washing up could be so much fun? Suzy didn't want it to end, but she saw the clock. Mum would be expecting her home.

Maybe she does care about you, then? Suzy didn't know where that thought came from.

Drying her hands, Aunty Elizabeth asked, 'Are you ready for me to drive you home?' Suzy nodded. 'Great, give me five minutes, and we'll go. But you must come again, you'll always be welcome.'

Suzy looked from Aunty Elizabeth to Izzy, and knew she would be.

While Aunty Elizabeth drove Suzy home, Izzy did her homework. She didn't have much today, just a bit of French vocabulary, and she'd finished it by the time Aunty Elizabeth got back.

'Did you give Suzy's mum your number?'

'Yes, I did,' Aunty Elizabeth put her hand on Izzy's shoulder. 'Suzy will be OK, Izzy. You're a good friend.' *You're a good niece, as well.* 'Now, if you've finished your homework, shall I make us some hot chocolate before bed?'

As they curled up on the sofa with **STEAMING** mugs of hot chocolate, in a house a few streets away, Suzy was already in bed. She was thinking about Izzy and her aunty. She'd had a great time with them, they were brilliant. And they believed in Jesus. Suzy frowned. That wasn't the right way to put it. They didn't just believe in him, he was their friend. They talked to him about normal things. Suzy yawned. She was too tired to think about it all now. 'Goodnight, Jesus, if you're there,' she whispered, and as she wondered if he was there and listening, she hoped he was. 'And please help me stop being a bully . . .'

'Right, time for bed,' Aunty Elizabeth finished the last of her hot chocolate.

This was the first night at Aunty Elizabeth's where Izzy had not gone to her room early.

'See you tomorrow.' Izzy put down her empty mug and gave her aunt a hug. *Please pick me up in your car after school*, she thought, but she didn't say that out loud.

When Izzy got to her room, there was Teddy on her bed. It was time to open another letter from Gran! Izzy changed into her pyjamas and reached for Teddy. Her finger traced over the '**Izzy**' that Gran had sewed on the bottom of Teddy's left foot. The first letter had been about getting to know Jesus. Izzy was getting to know him, and she was getting to know Aunty Elizabeth, too.

The second letter had been about giving what we can to help others. Izzy thought back to Kelly and the grass-buzz. Now Kelly was a good friend.

The third letter had been about noticing people. Izzy had noticed Suzy, and she'd learned that there was more to Aunty Elizabeth than it seemed.

The fourth letter had been about being a friend. Izzy and Katy were friends.

Izzy smiled.

Opening the little pocket in Teddy's jeans, Izzy pulled out the next envelope, opened it carefully, and began to read.

Dear Izzy

I can't stop thinking about that poor boy I told you about last time.

When I met Helen for coffee today, we were still talking about it.

What if Mrs Smith hadn't helped, I said, and they threw the boy in the freezer with the peas, as well as his bag?

Helen said but she did help, so there was no need to worry about that.

I said if I'd been there, I'd have told them to get lost.

Izzy smiled. Her gran would have done, as well!

Helen said if I did, I would be like Jesus. That surprised me, to be honest, Izzy. Helen said that Jesus always stuck up for people. She said that once, he was having dinner with some people, and a woman came and poured perfume on his head. I said, 'What?' Helen said that it was a way of showing that Jesus was special. But some of the others began to make fun of the woman, and not be nice to her, and say she was wasting money. Basically, they bullied her, Izzy. And Jesus told them to leave her alone.

I liked that, thinking that Jesus stuck up for people. If I ever see someone's bag being thrown in with the peas, I know what to do.

Love from Gran

Izzy folded the letter away. I'm sorry to disappoint you, Gran, but I really don't think you'll be seeing bags thrown in peas!

Climbing into bed, Izzy hugged Teddy, her fingers still tracing the 'Izzy' on his foot.

Before turning off the light, she wrote in her Word Book: Honest, CU, UNO.

Friday

The next morning at the breakfast table, Izzy said grace.

'**Jesus**,

Please help Aunty Elizabeth have a good day, and help me have a good time at CU, and let Mum and Dad and Gran be having a good holiday.

Amen.'

Not so long ago, Izzy couldn't wait for Mum and Dad to come home, so she didn't have to stay at Aunty Elizabeth's. Now she was praying they'd have a good time away. She missed them, but staying at Aunty Elizabeth's wasn't so bad, after all.

Izzy picked up a slice of toast, and saw Aunty Elizabeth watching her, with a smile. 'Did you forget something?'

Izzy didn't think so. And why wasn't Aunty Elizabeth eating her breakfast? Oh!

'Jesus,

Thank you for our food as well. Sorry I forgot!

Amen.'

Izzy and Aunty Elizabeth were laughing as they began to eat.

'What did you mean when you said CU?' asked Aunty Elizabeth as she spread more jam on her toast.

Izzy had forgotten that she hadn't told Aunty Elizabeth about CU.

'It stands for Christian Union. Katy told me about it. She said there are other people there who want to be Jesus' friend, and I just thought it might be good to go.'

'It sounds a bit like the youth group I went to.'

'Yes,' Izzy laughed, 'and my friend Lucy is just like you!'

'What do you mean?'

'Well, she didn't want to come with us to CU, but then Katy told her Gary would be there, and she changed her mind!'

'I see what you mean!'

After breakfast, Aunty Elizabeth went to work, and Izzy to school.

Turning the corner of the road school was on, Izzy felt three **TAPS** on her shoulder. It was Jo! She was all out of breath from running to catch up with Izzy. 'I . . . I . . . I . . .' Jo gasped, and the two girls laughed. Eventually, Jo managed to speak. 'I need to ask you if you want to come to the cinema in a few weeks? It's my brother's birthday. It'll be mostly his friends, and he'll probably pick a rubbish movie.' Jo wrinkled her nose, and Izzy laughed again. Jo loved her brother, but Izzy knew he annoyed her, too. 'So anyway,' Jo continued, 'Mum said I can take a friend. Will you come?'

Izzy stopped laughing. She hadn't told Jo how she felt when she saw Jo with Kelly. She hadn't told anyone, not even Jesus. Had Jo guessed? Izzy didn't think so.

Maybe it was Jesus. Maybe he knew how she felt, even without being told.

I do. But it's nice when you tell me, as well!

'Are you sure, Jo? Wouldn't you rather ask Kelly?'

'What? No. Kelly is great, but Mum said I can only take one friend, and you're my **best** friend, so . . . unless you'd rather hang out with Suzy now?'

Izzy shook her head.

'Suzy is great, but you're my best friend, Jo! Of course I want to come.'

They linked little fingers and Jo saw her watch. 'Oh no, I'm late for my flute lesson. See you later!' And she ran off towards school, her bag bumping up and down on her shoulder.

'Bye!' Izzy walked slowly in the same direction her friend had taken, kicking a stone and thinking.

Jesus knew how she felt? Even she hadn't known what the mixed up feeling inside was, but Jesus knew. *He must know me better than anyone, including me*, thought Izzy.

Looking up, she saw Katy and Kelly going in through the school gate, and jogged to catch them up.

The three girls walked up the drive together.

'Your hair looks good,' said Izzy. Katy had her hair pulled back in a ponytail today, not hiding her face.

They were nearly at the school entrance, when they heard a shout: 'Oi! Tomato! Strawberry!'

Charlie. Charlie was one of Suzy's gang. A few of them were hanging around the entrance, probably waiting for Suzy.

Izzy turned towards Katy, who had tears in her eyes. Her face was towards the ground, and she was pulling her hair out of its ponytail.

Jesus, what do I do? My friend is really upset.

Izzy remembered Gran's letter, about how Jesus stuck up for people.

Suzy's gang were beginning to leave, when Izzy's voice stopped them.

'Leave her alone.'

The gang stood still. No one ever spoke to them like that.

Charlie turned back. 'What did you say?'

Izzy gulped. 'I said, leave my **friend** alone.'

Katy peeped through her hair. 'Friend'? She managed a small smile through her tears. Yes, she had friends now.

'Do you want to come closer and say that?' Charlie raised her fist.

Izzy, Katy and Kelly stood in a line.

Charlie and her pals stood in a line opposite them.

'Come on,' jeered Charlie. 'Come over here, or are you too chicken?'

She and her friends made chicken noises.

Cluck cluck cluck.

Suzy arrived and looked back and forth between the two groups. 'What's going on?'

'She's trying to tell me what to do,' said Charlie. 'That's not on, is it, Suze?'

Charlie was confident Suzy would be on her side. Hadn't Suzy herself joked about Katy's face before? OK, so it was a bit weird yesterday when Suzy clapped for Katy in drama, but things would be back to normal today.

'Only cos you had a go at Katy,' said Izzy, defensively.

Suzy looked at Katy, who was hiding behind her hair. Suzy thought she was crying.

'What did you say to her, Charlie?'

'It was just about her face. Come on, Suze, let's go.'

Suzy knew Charlie expected her to agree, but she didn't move.

They were all quiet now, apart from little sniffles from Katy, as they watched Suzy.

Suzy stared hard at the ground. No one else knew it, but she was talking to Jesus.

Jesus, if you're even there, help me do the **RIGHT THING**. *Please.*

Slowly, Suzy started walking. Charlie's mouth fell open. Suzy was walking towards Izzy, Katy and Kelly.

'What are you doing, Suze?' spluttered Charlie. 'Is this a joke?'

'No. No one has said anything funny around here.'

Charlie turned a bit red at that.

'Um, OK, Suze. See you at lunchtime, in our usual place?'

She said 'our' very firmly. Izzy got the message.

'It's OK,' she said to Suzy, 'we have plans anyway. We're going to CU.'

'CU? Is that the Jesus club?' Charlie scoffed. Suzy knew what she was thinking: CU was for 𝕃𝕆𝕊𝔼ℝ𝕊.

Izzy nodded.

Suzy examined her fingernails, trying to look casual. 'Maybe I'll come with you.'

Charlie's eyes nearly popped out of her head.

'Are you serious, Suze?'

'Well, yeah, might as well give it a go. Something to do at lunchtime.'

Really, Suzy couldn't wait to go to CU, but she acted cool.

'You can come with us if you like, Charlie.'

Everyone looked at Katy.

Katy still had her hair in front of her face, and she put her head down as soon as she'd finished speaking, but she had definitely invited Charlie to come to CU.

'Are you serious? As if I'd go there!' Charlie looked at her gang for support.

'Yeah, right on, Charlie!' and they all put their hands to their foreheads, making an 'L' shape. Loser.

Charlie couldn't believe it. Suzy going to the Jesus club? There was no room in the gang for that sort of thing. Suzy was out. It was Charlie's gang now.

Charlie jerked her head, the way Suzy had always done to get the gang to follow her.

Suzy saw, and knew what it meant. She thought she should feel more than relief, but she didn't.

Charlie's gang walked off.

Jesus? Why don't they want to know you? Izzy didn't understand. She and Aunty Elizabeth wanted to know Jesus. Even her friends had said they would come to CU. And Jesus had been really helping this week. Why wouldn't anyone want to know him?

Some people don't. It's not your fault, Izzy. You can't make people want to know me. All you can do is give people the chance, which is what you're doing!

During the last lesson before lunch, Charlie's gang kept flicking little balls of paper at Izzy and her friends, especially Izzy. Izzy ignored them.

The clock ticked slowly but finally the lesson was over.

It was time for CU.

The girls met in the corridor outside the room where CU was held.

As they stood in a little circle in front of the door, they were **nervous**. Even Katy was nervous, although she'd been to CU before. What if she wasn't welcome back?

Izzy put her hand in the space in the middle of the group.

'Come on, we're together in this.'

One by one, the girls put their hands on top of Izzy's. The teams did this when they played netball in PE, to encourage each other.

'One, two, three . . . ' said Suzy. 'Let's go!' they said together, raising their hands up in the air.

Katy opened the door.

CU

The room was already full of people from all the year groups, including from the boys' school. Some Izzy recognized, some she didn't. They all stopped talking and turned to STARE as Katy led the group of girls in. When they saw Suzy, their eyes grew wide. Everyone knew about Bully Suzy.

Gary spoke first. 'Hi, Katy! Hi everyone, come in.'

They took off their coats and sat down. Izzy noticed that Lucy managed to take the seat beside Gary!

There was an awkward silence at first, but everyone soon began to chat as they ate their lunch.

The door opened and a man in leathers walked in. 'This is Sam,' said Gary. 'He goes to my church, and he's going to talk to us today.'

Gary went to church?

Everyone moved their chairs into a semicircle and Sam jumped up and sat on a table in front of them. He grinned, his teeth white next to his dark skin.

141

'I want to tell you about my mate Tim. I met Tim because of motorbikes. In case you hadn't guessed, I like bikes!' he pointed to his leathers.

'I was out on my bike one day about five years ago, and Tim was out on the road as well. He was in a lorry, and he didn't see me coming.'

Kelly put her hand to her mouth.

'Next thing I knew, I was lying in the road with part of my bike going from the back of my shoulder and sticking out of the other side.

'I heard sirens coming, and saw blue **flashing lights**, but the pain was so bad I fainted.

'I woke up in hospital with a bandage on my shoulder and no arm.'

Sam leaned forward, and one sleeve of his jacket hung loosely. There was no arm in it. How had they not noticed that?

Jo put her hand up.

'But I thought you said Tim is your mate?'

'Yes. That's right, he is.'

'Even though he made you lose your arm?'

'Yes.'

Jo shook her head. 'I don't know how you can be his mate. He chopped your arm off. I'd never be friends with someone who did that to me.'

'Shall I tell you how I did it?'

They all nodded.

'At first, I was really mad at him. I was in hospital for a long time and every day Tim phoned the hospital to check how I was doing. He always asked the nurses if he could speak to me, but I said no. Why would I want to speak to the person who ruined my life? So every day, I lay there in bed, thinking about Tim and what he'd done. I was really angry and depressed.

'One day, a vicar turned up on the ward. I went to church when I was a kid, but I stopped when I left home. The vicar was just visiting the patients, going from one to another. I watched him, and as he got nearer to me, I decided to tell him to **GET LOST**. I didn't want to talk to him, and I knew he wouldn't want to talk to me really – why would a vicar want to speak to someone who was angry at God?'

'You were angry at God?' someone from Year 10 spoke for them all.

'I was.'

'But . . . didn't he mind?' asked Gary.

Sam smiled. 'That's a great question. Do you know what? I don't think God did mind. He wants us to be honest. If I'd said, "I'm so glad my arm got chopped off" I reckon God would have known I was not telling the truth. Don't you?'

Everyone **laughed**.

Izzy thought of Jesus telling her to 'just be honest'. She thought of when she told him she was sad. Yes, God could cope with the truth.

'Anyway, the vicar came up to my bed, and I was about to tell him to go away when he offered me a chocolate. That took me by surprise and the next thing I knew, the vicar was sitting in the chair by my bed, unwrapping the chocolate for me. By the way, it is really hard to unwrap a chocolate with one hand!'

Izzy made a mental note to try it next time she had a chocolate.

'While I was eating the chocolate, the vicar started talking about the Bible.'

'Why didn't you stop him?' asked Jo.

'I couldn't! The toffee in the chocolate was sticking my teeth together, and I couldn't talk.'

More laughter.

'So there I was, one arm, teeth stuck together, and the vicar was talking about someone called Peter. I was thinking, what? Apparently, this Peter was feeling really bad, because he'd let his friend down. His friend was Jesus, and when Jesus was having a hard time, Peter had not stuck up for him. Peter had pretended he didn't even know him, just so Peter didn't get in trouble too.'

'What was the hard time?' wondered Izzy.

'Jesus had been accused of doing bad stuff. It was lies, Jesus never did anything wrong, but people believed the lies and they said Jesus had to be crucified.'

'What does cru- croo- that word mean?' Kelly struggled to say it.

'Crucified means being nailed to a cross and left to die.'

'Unbelievable!' muttered Suzy.

'What do you mean?' Sam looked at her.

'I mean Peter! Unbelievable that he would turn his back on someone in trouble like that.'

Suzy thought about earlier, when she'd had to choose which side to take. She was glad she'd chosen to stick up for Katy.

'No wonder Peter felt bad.' Jo folded her arms. 'Did Jesus actually die, though?'

'Yes, and three days later he came back to life! God made him alive again.'

Wow, thought Izzy, God can **RAISE** people from the **DEAD**! Then she realized she'd said it out loud, because Sam answered her.

'He can, that's right. Not long after that, Jesus went back to heaven, where he lives.'

Gran's letter said that's where he lives! This time Izzy didn't say it out loud.

'Here's a question,' said Sam. 'If you knew you were going away, what would you say to someone?'

'Um, how about "**bye**"?' suggested Suzy, and they all laughed. They'd relaxed a bit now they'd seen that Suzy was alright.

'What did Jesus say?' asked a boy with ginger hair.

'He said, "I'm with you all the time." And it's true. You can't see him, but he's here right now.'

'But I thought you said he's in heaven?' Kelly looked around. 'Our school is OK but I'm not sure it's heaven!'

They laughed again.

'It's a Jesus thing,' said Sam. 'Not a people thing. We might not be able to understand how he can be everywhere, but if Jesus said it, it must be true. He's here right now.'

Yes he is, thought Izzy. *Thank you, Jesus.*

'Sam, what happened about Peter?' Suzy wanted to know.

'One day, Peter was fishing with his friends, when he saw Jesus on the beach. So, he jumped out of the boat, and swam to Jesus to say hi.'

'After the way Peter had treated Jesus before, I bet Jesus told him where to go!' said Jo.

'Well, sort of. He said, "Let's go for a walk."'

'What, both of them?' Suzy looked disbelieving. 'I wouldn't have thought Jesus would want anything to do with Peter.'

'Yeah, I'm surprised Jesus didn't push Peter back in the sea!' Jo added.

'Yes, they both went for a walk, because Jesus wanted to ask Peter a question.'

'Was it, "Why"?' asked Izzy. 'Why did you pretend you didn't even know me?'

'Was it, "Who do you think you are, treating me the way you have"?' asked Jo.

'No,' said Sam, and he looked around the group. 'Anyone else want to have a guess?'

'Was it, "What"?' guessed Kelly. 'What do you think you're doing, coming up to me now?'

'No. Anyone else?'

They all shook their heads.

'Jesus' question was, "Do you **love** me?"'

The room was quiet.

Eventually Jo spoke. 'Well, that was a silly question, wasn't it?'

'Why do you say that, Jo?' asked Sam.

'Of course Peter didn't love him, or he wouldn't have treated him as he did. I mean, who pretends they don't even know their friend, just so they don't get into trouble?'

'We might think so, but Peter said, "Yes, I do love you."'

'I don't think Jesus would have believed him, though,' said Kelly, quietly.

'He did believe him. He gave him a **second chance**.'

'What do you mean?' asked Izzy.

'He said he still wanted Peter in his life, and even that Peter could help him.'

Izzy was thinking about Mum and Aunty Elizabeth.

'So, even though Peter did the wrong thing, Jesus still wanted to be friends with him?'

'Exactly!' said Sam. 'I couldn't have put it better myself.' He smiled at Izzy, and she smiled shyly back.

'What about the vicar?' remembered Jo.

'Oh yes. Well, he told me the story I've just told you, and somehow we ended up talking about what happened to me and the crash and Tim, and somewhere in it all I realized that maybe I should give Tim a second chance, like Jesus gave Peter.'

Sam saw the clock. 'It's nearly time for you to get to your lessons. Long story short, the next time Tim phoned the ward and the nurses asked me if I wanted to speak to him, I said yes. And that's how we became mates. I'll tell you more if I come again.'

They gathered up their bags and coats, and as they left, Sam said, 'Remember, sometimes people deserve a second chance. And remember, no matter what you do or how much you mess up, Jesus will always give you a second chance, just like he did for Peter.'

After school, as they walked to the gate, the gang agreed that they wanted to go to CU again next week.

Izzy saw Amy climbing into her aunty's car. It doesn't matter that Aunty Elizabeth doesn't meet me, she told herself, even though she knew it did matter really. Blinking back tears, Izzy shoved her hands in her coat pockets and kept her head down as she walked. She heard the 'BEEP' of a car horn, but she didn't look.

Photos

The horn beeped again, twice. Izzy looked up. Across the road, she saw a blue car. It had two seats, and everything inside it was white. Aunty Elizabeth had come! Izzy waved, then crossed the road and climbed in the car. She gave Aunty Elizabeth a hug: 'You came!'

They drove off, and Izzy waved to her friends. She couldn't stop smiling. Her aunty had met her after school!

Thank you, Jesus. He'd known. He'd known how much she wished Aunty Elizabeth would meet her after school.

Aunty Elizabeth asked Izzy if she had much homework.

The car roof was not down today, so Izzy heard her!

'I've only got a bit of geography.'

'Good,' said Aunty Elizabeth, 'because tonight is **pizza** night.'

Izzy smiled even wider. Aunty Elizabeth had met her from school and remembered pizza night.

When they got back to the flat, Izzy went to her room to do her geography. It didn't take long, and soon she headed to the kitchen. On her way out of the bedroom, she gave Teddy a pat on the head. She knew there was a letter to read later.

When she got to the kitchen, she helped herself to juice, and drank it all down straight away. Wiping her mouth, she put her empty glass in the sink. Where was Aunty Elizabeth?

Wandering into the sitting room, Izzy found her aunt on the sofa, surrounded by old photo albums.

Seeing Izzy, she moved some from the seat next to her. 'Come and sit down and have a look at these photos.'

They bent their heads together over the albums.

'Look at that one!' Izzy pointed. 'Is that Gran?'

'Yes, we were on holiday in Cornwall. I must have been about 8. I took that photo and I remember your mum was making me GIGGLE at the time, that's why the photo is a bit blurry!'

Izzy decided to be brave. 'So, you and Mum used to be friends?'

'Oh yes. We were like a little team. Sticking together all the time.'

Izzy wanted to ask what happened, but she wasn't that brave.

They continued looking at photos, and laughing over the clothes people wore back then, until Aunty Elizabeth went to put the pizza in the oven. 'While I'm gone, you choose a movie to watch, Izzy. We'll eat our pizza in here.'

Izzy chose one she'd not seen before, and soon they were sitting side by side, eating pizza and watching the movie.

'Great choice of movie, Izzy, I like this one.'

They liked the same movies, and the same pizza? Izzy was happy inside as she helped herself to another slice.

When the movie finished, Aunty Elizabeth picked up their plates. 'Now, how about some hot chocolate?'

Soon she was back, with two steaming mugs.

Izzy cradled the mug in her hands and curled her legs under her. 'I met someone with one arm today, at CU.'

'One arm?'

'Yes. He'd been knocked off his bike and now he's best friends with the person who made him lose his arm.'

'**REALLY**?' Aunty Elizabeth looked sceptical.

'Yes, really. It's true. He told us that Jesus believes in second chances, and this man decided to do the same. Jesus had a friend who let him down, but it didn't mean the friend didn't still love him. And Jesus gave him a second chance.'

'Was that friend called P something?'

'Yes, Peter.'

'That's right. You reminded me of hearing the story at youth group. I'd forgotten all about it. Peter let Jesus down big time, didn't he, and Jesus forgave him.'

Aunty Elizabeth was thoughtful. Looking at the photos with Izzy, and being reminded about second chances, had made her think about her sister. She couldn't even remember why they'd fallen out with each other.

Izzy picked up the photo album again and a loose photo slipped out. It was a photo of a little girl, and on the back was written the word 'Izzy'.

'Why am I in your photo album?'

Aunty Elizabeth took the photo, and her finger traced the writing on the back.

Eventually, she said, 'You're not, Izzy. This is me.'

'What?'

'Everyone used to call me Izzy. I think "Elizabeth" was a bit of a mouthful sometimes, so I became Izzy. I was only ever called Elizabeth when someone told me off!'

Izzy's forehead **wrinkled**.

'Aunty Elizabeth? Did you fall out with my mum before or after I was born?'

'What's that got to do with anything?'

'Just tell me.'

'It was before. A long time before you were born.'

'So, even though Mum and you weren't speaking to each other, she chose to call her baby after you?'

Aunty Elizabeth just nodded.

'But . . . ' something in Aunty Elizabeth's face made Izzy stop talking.

She looked back at the photo for a long time, then she stood up. 'I think I'll go to bed now. Thank you for the pizza and for meeting me after school.'

Izzy hugged her aunt, and went to her bedroom.

Aunty Elizabeth stayed where she was, thinking back over the evening.

Izzy had said Peter still loved Jesus, even though Peter let Jesus down. And Jesus gave him a second chance. Aunty Elizabeth had forgotten that her sister called her baby 'Izzy' even after the falling out. Maybe there is still some love there? Maybe. She looked at her watch. They'd be home from holiday now, and it wasn't too late . . .

She picked up the phone and called her sister. 'Hello, Sally. It's Elizabeth.'

'Elizabeth?'

'Yes. Izzy . . . '

In her bedroom, Izzy reached for Teddy. It was time to open the next letter. The first letter had been about getting to know Jesus. Izzy was getting to know him, and she was getting to know Aunty Elizabeth, too.

The second letter had been about giving what we can to help others. Izzy thought back to Kelly and the grass buzz. Now Kelly was a good friend.

The third letter had been about noticing people. Izzy had noticed Suzy, and she'd learned that there was more to Aunty Elizabeth than it seemed.

The fourth letter had been about being a friend. Izzy and Katy were friends.

The fifth letter had been about inside being more important than outside.

What would the next one be about?

Dear Izzy

It's Helen's birthday soon, and I said we should celebrate. Last year on her birthday, I didn't know her!

Helen said that celebrating reminded her of a story Jesus told.

Izzy was learning that Jesus was in everything!

The story is about a man who was really rich. He owned lots of land, and he had two sons who helped him look after it. One day, the youngest son was really fed up and grumpy. He didn't want to work on his dad's land anymore, so he left.

His dad was really sad, he missed his son. Every day he looked out for his son, hoping he would come back. But he never did.

Finally, the son did come back and his dad was so happy he threw a party! The son kept saying, 'But what about what I did? I ran away, I didn't want to speak to you.'

And the dad said, 'It doesn't matter now. All that matters is that you are home.'

Isn't that great?

Love Gran

Climbing into bed, Izzy reached for her Word Book: Peter, Photos, Izzy.

She hesitated over the last word. Was it OK to put Izzy? Settling down to sleep, Izzy decided that it was. 'Izzy' had been an important word today.

Saturday

The next morning, Izzy woke up and remembered it was Saturday. No school today! Had she really been at Aunty Elizabeth's for a whole week?

Last Saturday, she'd stood on the doorstep of this flat and wanted to run away.

So much had happened since then.

Grass buzz, chocolate buttons, playing UNO, pizza . . .

'thank you, Jesus,' she whispered. 'Everything is better since I met you.'

She got out of bed, washed and dressed, then went to the kitchen. Aunty Elizabeth was already there, flicking through a recipe book.

'Morning, Izzy. Good timing. Help yourself to some breakfast, and then I thought we could bake some cakes.'

'Bake some cakes?' repeated Izzy. She didn't even know Aunty Elizabeth knew how to bake!

'Yes. I thought it would be fun.'

'Fun?'

'And we have a visitor coming later.'

'A visitor?'

Izzy was beginning to feel like a parrot.

'Yes, that's right. The only thing is, I've not baked for years.'

'I can help,' said Izzy. 'I bake cakes with Gran, I know what to do. The first thing is to put aprons on.' She looked doubtfully around the kitchen. Did Aunty Elizabeth even have one apron, let alone two?

But Aunty Elizabeth opened a drawer and took out two aprons. As they tied them round their waists, Izzy said, 'At Gran's, my apron has my name on. Gran sewed it on for me.'

Aunty Elizabeth stopped still.

'Is your name sewed onto a red heart?'

'How did you know that?'

Aunty Elizabeth cleared her throat. 'Because it used to be **my apron**. Your gran made it for me. She must have kept it.'

They finished tying their aprons, and looked at each other.

'When you put your aprons on,' began Izzy, 'did Gran always . . . '

'Give me a hug?' Aunty Elizabeth remembered those hugs. 'Yes.'

'Me too.'

'I think we should carry on the tradition!' Aunty Elizabeth crossed the kitchen and gave Izzy a big hug.

'Me too,' Izzy hugged her back. '**definitely**.'

Aunty Elizabeth put some music on, and they started mixing the cakes. When the mixture was ready, they poured it into the cake cases, ready to put in the oven. Gran usually scraped all the mix into the cases, but Aunty Elizabeth left a lot in the bowl. When the cakes were in the oven, she handed Izzy a spoon. 'Come on, this is the best bit.'

They sat together at the table, scraping out the cake mix from the bowl and eating it. Gran never let Izzy do that! Aunty Elizabeth had flour in her hair and on her nose. Izzy giggled, and Aunty Elizabeth joined in.

When the cakes were ready, they decorated them with icing and colourful sprinkles. Just as they finished, they heard the sound of the doorbell.

Aunty Elizabeth looked nervous. She brushed the flour from her hair and nose, and took her apron off. Straightening her back, she went to answer the door.

As Izzy was taking her own apron off, she heard voices. Surely that wasn't MUM'S voice? Mum was coming to pick her up to go home today, but not until later. Mum being here already would spoil the time with Aunty Elizabeth's visitor. So embarrassing. When the visitor arrived, it would be really awkward if they all had to sit there with Aunty Elizabeth and Mum not speaking to each other.

How was she going to get Mum to leave? All Izzy could think of was to say that she would leave too, but Izzy wanted to stay and meet Aunty Elizabeth's visitor.

She was trying to work out what to do, when Mum walked into the kitchen, followed by Aunty Elizabeth. Oh no. Izzy's heart started to beat faster. She was sure everyone could hear it.

Mum came and gave her a hug. 'Hi, Izzy! I'm told you've been making cakes? I can't wait to try one.' Mum smiled, first at Izzy, then at Aunty Elizabeth. Aunty Elizabeth smiled back.

Izzy looked from one to another. Was she dreaming?

Later, when they were in the sitting room, talking and eating cake, Mum spotted the photo album. She and Aunty Elizabeth flicked through it together, laughing at the memories.

Izzy watched them. Were they friends again? Or what?

'Mum?'

Mum looked up. 'Yes?'

'Why did you call me Izzy?'

The room went very quiet.

'Because,' Mum glanced at Aunty Elizabeth, 'Izzy is not only my sister, she's my best friend. I just forgot it for a while.'

When it was time to leave, Izzy fetched her bag from her bedroom, then had to turn back. She'd almost forgotten Teddy! There was one unopened letter in his pocket, and Izzy would open that later.

At the front door, Aunty Elizabeth **hugged** them both. Such a change from when she wouldn't even look at them!

Thank you, Jesus.

'Bye! See you tomorrow!'

In the car, Izzy asked Mum what happened with her and Aunty Elizabeth.

'That's the thing, we can't really remember! I expect one of us said something, and the other one was upset, and we never sorted it out.'

Mum can't remember what happened? thought Izzy. *That's a bit like in Gran's letter, where the dad said that the only thing that mattered was that his son was home.*

Mum carried on, 'I remember a Bible verse I once heard: 'When you are angry, do not sin. And do not go on being angry all day.' It basically means put things right with people before the end of the day. It's a good verse, and I wish I'd followed it. Izzy and I wasted too much time being angry with each other.'

Izzy? Izzy was about to say that she wasn't angry, then remembered Mum meant Aunty Elizabeth. Or maybe 'Aunty Izzy' now!

'Mum? How do you know a Bible verse? Did you go to the same youth group as Aunty Elizabeth?'

'Yes, I did. We went together.'

More surprises.

'Mum?' Izzy had one more question.

'Why did Aunty Elizabeth say she'd see us tomorrow?'

Mum glanced at Izzy, then turned her eyes back to the road.

'We thought we'd go to **church**. Is that OK with you?'

Izzy sat back in her seat and smiled. *Thank you, Jesus.* It was very OK with her.

At home, Izzy unpacked her case and was about to open the last letter from Gran, when she heard Dad. He was back from taking Gran to her house.

She ran down the stairs, taking two at a time, and jumped to hug him.

'Hi, Izzy-Bizzy!' Dad tweaked her nose. 'I missed you!'

It's a miracle!

When the three of them sat down to dinner, Izzy looked at Mum, then at Dad. They never said grace. She felt a bit embarrassed to ask, but thanking Jesus for his present of food had become important to her. She asked if she could say grace.

Mum smiled and nodded. Dad put his knife and fork down.

'Jesus,

Thank you that Mum and Aunty Elizabeth are friends again.

And thank you for our food.

Amen.'

'You and your sister have *MADE UP*?' Dad was incredulous.

Mum nodded.

'What a relief. Now you've got your best friend back. Izzy, you're a miracle worker!'

I'm not the miracle worker, am I, Jesus? But thank you that you are.

It was true. Izzy began to eat her potatoes, and thanked Jesus for making everything better. Even the hard things, like bullies at school, were easier to manage when she had Jesus with her.

Izzy smiled as she remembered how scared she'd been to talk to Suzy. And now she was going round to Suzy's house next week!

'How was your holiday?' she asked Mum and Dad. 'And Gran?'

'It was great, and Gran had a brilliant time. She is fine. Much better. The doctor was right that a holiday would do her good.'

Izzy still didn't know what was wrong with Gran, but she was glad Gran was getting better.

'She sends you her love, and says she is looking forward to seeing you. She says you will have LOTS to talk about.'

Izzy smiled. They certainly would!

'And what about you, Izzy?' Dad wondered. 'I know you didn't want to go to stay with your aunt. Thank you for doing it, though. Don't worry, we won't ask you to go again soon.'

'I wouldn't mind. Aunty Elizabeth is alright. Did you know she likes pizza? And she has a car with only two seats!'

She could see Dad was puzzled. What she didn't know was he was thinking she was exactly like his Izzy, and yet she was different somehow.

Later, when Izzy said goodnight, Mum reminded her about church tomorrow.

As if Izzy would forget!

'We need to leave just before 10 a.m., so we can pick Aunty Elizabeth up on the way.'

'OK,' said Izzy, and she turned her head. 'You can come, too, Dad, if you like.'

Dad coughed. 'No, thanks, Izzy, I don't think it's for me.'

Izzy thought of Charlie and her pals making the 'L for loser' sign. At least Dad wasn't doing that! And Jesus had said you can't make anyone want to get to know him, you can just give them a chance to.

'OK, Dad. But if you ever change your mind . . . '

As Izzy climbed the stairs to her bedroom, she whispered to Jesus, '**Please** let Dad change his mind one day. I really want him to be your friend, too.'

In her room, Teddy was waiting. There was one more letter to open!

Izzy changed into her pyjamas, climbed into bed, and began to read.

Dear Izzy

Helen and I went out for coffee today. It was at a really posh place, where they keep coming and filling your cup. 'Bottomless coffee', they called it. We drank all we wanted, our cups were never empty for long.

When we were on our third cup, I said to Helen that whoever invented bottomless coffee was a genius. You know how annoying I find it when you're given a cup the size of a thimble, and that's it, don't you, Izzy?

Izzy remembered times in cafés where Gran complained about the small cups. Yes, Gran, I do!

Helen said the coffee not running out reminded her of something that happened to Jesus. He was at a wedding once, and all the wine ran out. That would have been really embarrassing for the hosts. But Jesus turned water into wine, and the party carried on.

Do you know what I think, Izzy? Jesus makes everything better; even good things are better when he is around.

I've noticed that, too, Gran!

I told Helen, and she agreed. She also said that, a bit like the bottomless coffee, Jesus' besters – Helen called them blessings, but I think besters is a good word – never run

> *out. He always gives good things and there*
> *are always more to come.*
>
> *Love from Gran*

Izzy folded the letter and put it back in Teddy's pocket with the others. Besters was a good way to put it. She agreed with Gran; Jesus' besters were definitely the best!

She picked up her Word Book, wondering what words to use today. Cake? Surprises? Friends? Church? It had been a brilliant day.

That was it.

Izzy wrote one word: 'Brilliant!!!'

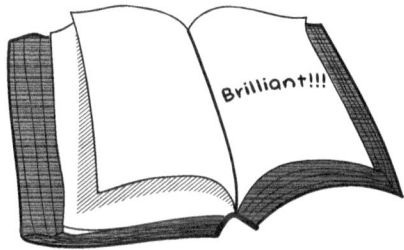

The last time she wrote one word was right at the beginning. Izzy flipped back through the pages until she found 'Rubbish' underlined three times beside an angry face.

A lot had changed since then.

Closing the book, Izzy lay down and turned off the light.

Jesus,

Thank you for making everything better.

Amen.

Sunday

When Izzy woke up the next morning, she wondered where she was. The room wasn't white! Then she remembered that she wasn't at Aunty Elizabeth's now, but she'd see her soon. They were going to church today!

Just before 10 a.m., Izzy and Mum called 'Bye!' to Dad, and set off in the car to collect Aunty Elizabeth. They couldn't go in Aunty Elizabeth's car, because they wouldn't all fit!

When they got to the church, Izzy suddenly felt **nervous**. She was glad Mum and Aunty Elizabeth were with her.

She wasn't nervous for long. Everyone in the church was really friendly and relaxed. Izzy saw Sam across the room, talking to a man who had a ponytail. Maybe that was Tim. At 10.30, someone stood on the stage at the front of the room, and everyone began to find a seat. Izzy pulled Mum and Aunty Elizabeth towards three seats together. The man on the stage welcomed everyone and explained that when there were songs to sing, the words would be on a big screen at the front. He gave a special welcome to anyone who was there for the first time. Izzy nudged Mum on one side, and Aunty Elizabeth on the other. That was them!

The band started playing some music, and Izzy saw Gary there. She didn't know he played guitar! Wait till she told Lucy.

The band played a few songs, and people joined in singing. Then the man on the stage, who was called Paul, started reading out loud from his **bible**.

It was the same story as the one in Gran's letter, the one about the wedding where Jesus turned water into wine!

Izzy remembered that all the stories in the letters were from the Bible, and that there were no more letters in Teddy's pocket.

She looked at the Bible in Paul's hand. It was quite big. There must be lots of things about Jesus that she didn't know.

Izzy decided that she was going to get a Bible of her own as soon as she could, so she could read more about Jesus.

After he'd read from the Bible, Paul started talking about the story.

When the wine ran out, people at the party asked Jesus to help.

'We can always ask Jesus to help us,' said Paul.

Izzy nodded. Jesus had helped her this week. She thought of how he helped her notice people, and make new friends, and get to know Aunty Elizabeth, and be brave and stand up for what was right.

'Secondly, blessings never run out with Jesus. He always has good things to give.'

There was that word again. '**blessings**.'

Well, decided Izzy, whether they are called blessings or besters, I like them!

She linked arms with Mum and Aunty Elizabeth.

Thank you, Jesus.

Epilogue

Izzy picked up the phone and called Gran. It went straight to voicemail. Gran was probably out somewhere with Helen. Izzy decided to leave a message; hopefully Gran would remember to listen to it!

'Hi Gran! Thank you for the letters in Teddy. They introduced me to Jesus, and now he is my friend, too. I am going to get a Bible so I can read more about him myself. Bye for now.'

Two days later, a parcel arrived for Izzy. She opened it, and inside was a Bible. It was from Gran! There was a note:

Dear Izzy

This Bible is full of *besters*.

Enjoy it.

And I think Teddy would like to live with you now.

Love from Gran

Izzy put the Bible beside Teddy on her bed.

She saw the word '𝕀ℤℤ𝕐' on his foot. Had Teddy once belonged to Aunty Elizabeth, like the apron had?

Izzy must remember to ask Aunty Elizabeth next time she saw her. They had lots of 'getting to know more about each other' to do.

Just as they had more things to learn and know about Jesus.

More besters.

Izzy could hardly wait.

But she didn't need to wait!

Picking up her new Bible, Izzy saw a bookmark sticking out.

She was about to open the page marked, when she heard Mum's voice coming up the stairs: 'Izzy! Gran's on the phone for you!'

Mum opened Izzy's door. Izzy took the phone and lay down on her bed. 'Hi, Gran!'

'Hi, Izzy! Sorry I missed your call the other day, I was at church helping in the garden.'

'That's OK! I just wanted to say thanks for the letters. Thank you for the Bible, too.'

'You're welcome. Enjoy it!'

'Thanks, I will.'

Izzy paused. 'Gran? Do you ever think what if?'

'What if what?'

Izzy couldn't think how to say it. Gran tried to help her out. 'Do you mean things like, "What if the sky was green with yellow spots?" Or, "what if carrots were blue?" Or . . . '

Izzy smiled and rolled her eyes. 'No, Gran, I don't mean that! I mean things like Jo still being my best friend, or Aunty Elizabeth picking me up in her car. I mean, I really wanted those things to happen, and they did. I think Jesus knew I wanted them to happen, and helped them happen.'

Gran didn't say anything, but Izzy could tell she was listening.

'But what if they hadn't happened? What if Jo stopped being my friend, or if Aunty Elizabeth didn't come? Or what if Dad never wants to be Jesus' friend? Would I . . . '
Izzy broke off.

'Would you what, darling?' asked Gran, gently.

'Would it mean Jesus wasn't my friend? Would it mean he didn't love me anymore?' Izzy whispered.

'Hug,' said Gran, and Izzy knew Gran was imagining giving her a hug. Imagined hugs were the next best thing to real ones. 'When I was at church the other day, Izzy,

I had to go inside to get the gardening tools. As I came out, I saw a picture above the door. It was a verse from the Bible.'

Just then, there was a noise in the background, and Izzy missed the beginning of what Gran said. She heard '. . . can separate us from the love God has for us.'

'What?' Izzy sat up in a panic. 'What did you say can separate us from his love?'

She knew it. If her what ifs didn't work out, it would mean Jesus didn't love her anymore. Izzy didn't want her what ifs not to work out, but even more she didn't want Jesus to stop loving her. And now Gran was saying something could make that happen.

'What?' said Izzy again. 'Tell me!'

'Nothing,' said Gran.

'Tell me!' said Izzy 'Please, Gran. Don't just say nothing, like it doesn't matter.'

Gran laughed. 'I'm not saying "nothing, like it doesn't matter"! The opposite, Izzy. This "nothing" matters a lot. It means that NOTHING can stop Jesus loving you.'

Izzy's mouth dropped open slightly.

Nothing can stop it.

'Nothing,' Izzy whispered and, as she said goodbye to Gran, she was smiling.

Opening her Bible at the page with the bookmark sticking out, Izzy saw the word 'John' at the top of the page. The man at church had said he was reading from 'The book of John' when he read about Jesus turning water into wine. Izzy flipped through her Bible. It looked as though it was **lots** of books in one! All the books had chapters, and the chapters had numbers in them. Oh no, not more maths. But then she remembered that the man at church had called the numbers 'verses'. It was just a way to keep your place. Maybe verses were a bit like a bookmark? Even though they were numbers, if they were really just like bookmarks, that was OK.

She grabbed the phone and called Gran back.

'Gran, where is that bit about "nothing" and God's love in the Bible?'

'Romans 8 verse 38.'

'Thanks, Gran. Bye!'

As Gran put the phone down, she was smiling. Who'd have thought she and Izzy would be talking about the Bible?

Turning back to John, Izzy began to read:

Before the world began, there was the Word. The Word was with God, and the Word was God. He was with God in the beginning. All things were made through him. Nothing was made without him. In him there was life. That life was light for the people of the world. The Light shines in the darkness. And the darkness has not overpowered the Light.

John 1:1–5

Izzy read the beginning of the chapter three times. Chapter one, bookmarks – oops, verses! – 1–5.

What did it mean?

'The Word was with God . . .' Izzy scrabbled back through Teddy's letters. Yes, Gran had said, 'Jesus is the Son of God, the image of God.' 'Word' must be another name for Jesus. Maybe Jesus had more than one name, a bit like Dad called her Izzy-Bizzy. And even before the world began, Jesus was there.

'. . . and the Word was God.' Izzy's eyes opened wide. That must mean that Jesus was God! Wow! But what did the rest mean? Izzy twirled her hair round her finger as she read it again: 'Before the world began, there was the Word.'

Reading 'Word' reminded her of her Word Book. She hadn't wanted to keep a Word Book, and had only done so because Mrs James had told them to. They could stop now if they wanted, that piece of work was over, but Izzy thought she might carry on with hers. It had helped her make sense of her days.

Not as much as Jesus helped, though, and now she'd discovered 'the Word' was one of his names!

Izzy had an idea. She rummaged around in her desk drawer until she found a nearly new notebook. She tore out the two or three pages at the start where she'd doodled, and then wrote on the first page: 'Bible Word Book'. Then she wrote John chapter 1 verses 1–5 and underlined it with her pink sparkly pen. She would choose three words from that bit; maybe that would help her understand.

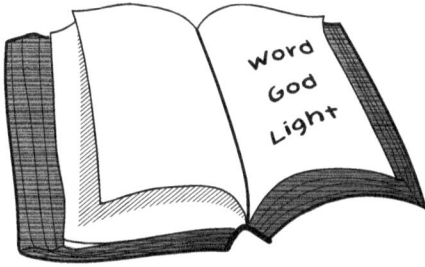

Chewing the end of her pen, Izzy slowly read the words again, and wrote: Word, God, Light.

The Light? It looked as though that was another name for Jesus. He seemed to have more names than anyone else Izzy knew!

Light in the darkness. Izzy buried her head under the duvet. It was dark in there, but there was no light. Emerging from the duvet, Izzy sat cross-legged on the bed and frowned.

'Light in the darkness.'

Light that gives life.

Izzy sat up a bit straighter. Her mind raced over the past week. There had been dark times, when things were hard, and they'd been better because of Jesus. Maybe *that* was what 'Light . . . in the darkness' meant; that Jesus made life better.

Izzy drew two columns:

Dark	Light
Going to Aunty Elizabeth's	Having a good time
Kelly on her own	Kelly joining The Gang
Suzy being a bully	Suzy becoming less mean
Me feeling sad	Jesus understanding
Katy hating the way she looks	Learning that inside is more important
Nervous about going to CU	Had a great time
Katy being bullied	Courage to stick up for her
Mum and Aunty E not speaking	Friends again

Light.

The 'L' reminded Izzy of another 'L' word – 'Love'.

She picked up her Bible. Near the beginning, she found a list of all the books in the Bible. Gran had said 'Romans'. Starting at the first book in the list – Genesis – Izzy ran her finger down until she found Romans. Page 1312. Then she found chapter 8, then verse 38.

'Nothing can separate us from the love God has for us.'

With her sparkly pink pen, Izzy underlined the word 'NOTHING'.

Izzy and Me

Izzy and Me

Chapter 1 – Friday

What's your favourite smell?

Izzy	Me
The sea	

Have you ever had to do something you didn't want to do?

Izzy	Me
Go and stay with Aunty Elizabeth	

Where do you feel safe?

Izzy	Me
At Gran's house	

Word Book

Izzy	Me
Rubbish!	

Izzy and Me

Chapter 2 – Saturday

Have you ever had a good surprise?

Izzy	Me
Finding letters in Teddy	

Why was it a good surprise?

Izzy	Me
Made me feel less alone	

Do you share a favourite thing with anyone?

Izzy	Me
Pizza, with Aunty Elizabeth	

Izzy and Me

Gran's letter said that Jesus is with us all the time. How do you feel about this?

Izzy	Me
At first I thought it was a weird idea, but now I 87 per cent think it might be true. It will be nice to have a friend with me, especially at the moment because I am on my own.	

Word Book

Izzy	Me
Tears	
Teddy	
Pizza	

Izzy and Me

Chapter 3 – Sunday

Is there someone who has helped you do things?

Izzy	Me
Aunty Elizabeth helped me make grass buzz	

Do you know that Jesus loves you? Or are you not sure?

Izzy	Me
I've never really thought about it before but Gran's letter said he does, so I think it's true that he does.	

Word Book

Izzy	Me
Duvet Grass-buzz Presents	

Remember Izzy discovered that all the stories in Gran's letters were in the Bible? Well, here they are. If you have a Bible, you could look them up for yourself. The bit to look for is in bold below.

Why don't you try choosing three words from each story? And think about the questions. Remember: there are no wrong answers!

Here's the story you read in Chapter 3. It's in the Bible:

John 6:5–14

Jesus looked up and saw a large crowd coming toward him. He said to Philip, 'Where can we buy bread for all these people to eat?' (Jesus asked Philip this question to test him. Jesus already knew what he planned to do.)

Philip answered, 'Someone would have to work almost a year to buy enough bread for each person here to have only a little piece.'

Another follower there was Andrew. He was Simon Peter's brother. Andrew said, 'Here is a boy with five loaves of barley bread and two little fish. But that is not enough for so many people.'

Jesus said, 'Tell the people to sit down.' This was a very grassy place. There were about 5,000 men who sat down there. Then Jesus took the loaves of bread. He thanked God for the bread and gave it to the people who were sitting there. He did the same with the fish. He gave them as much as they wanted.

They all had enough to eat. When they had finished, Jesus said to his followers, 'Gather the pieces of fish and bread that were not eaten. Don't waste anything.' So they gathered up the pieces that were left. They filled 12 large baskets with the pieces that were left of the five barley loaves.

The people saw this miracle that Jesus did. They said, 'He must truly be the Prophet who is coming into the world.'

Pick three words about the story above:

-

-

-

What did you learn about Jesus in the story?

Izzy and Me

Chapter 4 – Monday

Do you like maths?

Izzy	Me
NO!!!!!!!!	

Do you ever say grace before you eat?

Izzy	Me
I have two times, I only started today.	

How have you helped someone?

Izzy	Me
I helped Kelly make grass buzz and I made friends with her	

Word Book

Izzy	Me
Grace Kelly Maths	

Here's the story you read in Chapter 4. It's in the Bible:

Luke 8:42b–48

While Jesus was on his way to Jairus' house, the people were crowding all around him. A woman was there who had been bleeding for 12 years. She had spent all her money on doctors, but no doctor was able to heal her. The woman came up behind Jesus and touched the edge of his coat. At that moment, her bleeding stopped. Then Jesus said, 'Who touched me?'

All the people said they had not touched Jesus. Peter said, 'Master, the people are all around you and are pushing against you.'

But Jesus said, 'Someone did touch me! I felt power go out from me.' When the woman saw that she could not hide, she came forward, shaking. She bowed down before Jesus. While all the people listened, she told why she had touched him. Then, she said, she was healed immediately. Jesus said to her, 'Dear woman, you are healed because you believed. Go in peace.'

Pick three words

-

-

-

What did you learn about Jesus?

Izzy and Me

Chapter 5 – Tuesday

Have you ever been bullied?

Izzy	Me
Yes. Suzy bullies everyone.	

Suzy was mean because she was not happy inside. How do you feel inside?

Izzy	Me
Sometimes I am happy, but not always. I wish I was happy all the time.	

Maybe you could tell Jesus, just like Izzy did when she felt sad.

Word Book

Izzy	Me
Nervous	
Happy	
Sad	

Here's the story you read in Chapter 5. It's in the Bible:

Luke 19:1–10

Jesus was going through the city of Jericho. In Jericho there was a man named Zacchaeus. He was a wealthy, very important tax collector. He wanted to see who Jesus was, but he was too short to see above the crowd. He ran ahead to a place where he knew Jesus would come. He climbed a sycamore tree so he could see Jesus. When Jesus came to that place, he looked up and saw Zacchaeus in the tree. He said to him, 'Zacchaeus, hurry and come down! I must stay at your house today.'

Zacchaeus came down quickly. He was pleased to have Jesus in his house. All the people saw this and began to complain, 'Look at the kind of man Jesus stays with. Zacchaeus is a sinner!'

But Zacchaeus said to the Lord, 'I will give half of my money to the poor. If I have cheated anyone, I will pay that person back four times more!'

Jesus said, 'Salvation has come to this house today. This man truly belongs to the family of Abraham. The Son of Man came to find lost people and save them.'

Pick three words

-

-

-

What did you learn about Jesus?

Izzy and Me

Chapter 6 – Wednesday

What's your favourite thing about you on the outside?

Izzy	Me
My long hair.	

What's your favourite thing about you on the inside?

Izzy	Me
I am friendly.	

When you meet people, do you see that inside matters more than outside?

Izzy	Me
I think I am learning to.	

Who would you talk to if you were worried about someone?

Izzy	Me
An adult. When I was worried about Katy, I talked to Aunty Elizabeth.	

Izzy and Me

Word Book

Izzy	Me
Brave	
Mimicking	
Talking	

Here's the story you read in Chapter 6. It's in the Bible:

1 Samuel 16:1–13

The Lord said to Samuel, 'How long will you continue to feel sorry for Saul? I have rejected him as king of Israel. Fill your container with olive oil and go. I am sending you to Jesse who lives in Bethlehem. I have chosen one of his sons to be king.'

But Samuel said, 'If I go, Saul will hear the news. And he will try to kill me.'

The Lord said, 'Take a young calf with you. Say, "I have come to offer a sacrifice to the Lord." Invite Jesse to the sacrifice. Then I will show you what to do. You must appoint the one I show you.'

Samuel did what the Lord told him to do. When he arrived at Bethlehem, the elders of Bethlehem shook with fear. They met him and asked, 'Are you coming in peace?'

Samuel answered, 'Yes, I come in peace. I have come to make a sacrifice to the Lord. Make yourselves holy for the Lord and come to the sacrifice with me.' Then he made Jesse and his sons holy for the Lord. And he invited them to come to the sacrifice.

When they arrived, Samuel saw Eliab. Samuel thought, 'Surely the Lord has appointed this person standing here before him.'

But the Lord said to Samuel, 'Don't look at how handsome Eliab is. Don't look at how tall he is. I have not chosen him. God does not see the same way people see. People look at the outside of a person, but the Lord looks at the heart.'

Then Jesse called Abinadab and told him to pass by Samuel. But Samuel said, 'The Lord has not chosen this man either.' Then Jesse had Shammah pass by. But Samuel said, 'No, the Lord has not chosen this one.' Jesse had seven of his sons pass by Samuel. But Samuel said to him, 'The Lord has not chosen any of these.'

Then he asked Jesse, 'Are these all the sons you have?'

Jesse answered, 'I still have the youngest son. He is out taking care of the sheep.'

Samuel said, 'Send for him. We will not sit down to eat until he arrives.'

So Jesse sent and had his youngest son brought in. He was a fine boy, tanned and handsome.

The Lord said to Samuel, 'Go! Appoint him. He is the one.'

So Samuel took the container of olive oil. Then he poured oil on Jesse's youngest son to appoint him in front of his brothers. From that day on, the Lord's Spirit entered David with power. Samuel then went back to Ramah.

Pick three words

-

-

-

What did you learn about God?

Izzy and Me

Chapter 7 – Thursday

Who could you encourage?

Izzy	Me
Katy. My friends and I encouraged her in drama and hopefully we can do more.	

Would you go to CU?

Izzy	Me
Yes, because I want to find out more about Jesus and meet other people who are his friends too.	

Suzy was surprised that people could chat to Jesus in normal language, like to a friend. Have you tried chatting to Jesus like that?

Izzy	Me
Yes.	

Izzy and Me

What would you say to Jesus right now?

_ _

Word Book

Izzy	Me
Honest	
CU	
UNO	

Here's the story you read in Chapter 7. It's in the Bible:

Mark 14:3–9

Jesus was in Bethany. He was at dinner in the house of Simon, who had a harmful skin disease. While Jesus was there, a woman came to him. She had an alabaster jar filled with very expensive perfume, made of pure nard. The woman opened the jar and poured the perfume on Jesus' head.

Some of those who were there saw this and became angry. They complained to each other, saying, 'Why waste that perfume? It was worth a full year's work. It could be sold, and the money could be given to the poor.' They spoke to the woman sharply.

Jesus said, 'Don't bother the woman. Why are you troubling her? She did a beautiful thing for me. You will always have the poor with you. You can help them anytime you want. But you will not always have me. This woman did the only thing she could do for me. She poured perfume on my body. She did this before I die to prepare me for burial. I tell you the truth. The Good News will be told to people in all the world. And in every place it is preached, what this woman has done will be told. And people will remember her.'

Pick three words

-

-

-

What did you learn about Jesus?

Izzy and Me

Chapter 8 – Friday

Do you think it was brave to stick up for Katy in front of Charlie?

Izzy	Me
It felt brave when I did it!	

Can you unwrap a chocolate with one hand?

Izzy	Me
I don't know but next time I have a chocolate to unwrap, I will find out!	

If you were Sam, would you have made friends with Tim?

Izzy	Me
I hope so, but to be honest, I don't know.	

Are you surprised that Jesus forgave Peter?

Izzy	Me
Yes and no. Yes, because Peter did something really bad but no, because Jesus is nicer than anyone I have ever met.	

Izzy and Me

Who do you look like? Anyone in your family? Or a celebrity?

Izzy	Me
The people I look like most in my family are Mum and Aunty Elizabeth.	

Word Book

Izzy	Me
Peter	
Photos	
Izzy	

Here's the story you read in Chapter 8. It's in the Bible:

Luke 15:11–24

Then Jesus said, 'A man had two sons. The younger son said to his father, "Give me my share of the property." So the father divided the property between his two sons. Then the younger son gathered up all that was his and left. He traveled far away to another country. There he wasted his money in foolish living. He spent everything that he had. Soon after that, the land became very dry, and there was no rain. There was not enough food to eat anywhere in the country. The son was hungry and needed money. So he got a job with one of the citizens there. The man sent the son into the fields to feed pigs. The son was so hungry that he was willing to eat the food the pigs were eating. But no one gave him anything. The son realized that he had been very foolish. He thought, "All of my father's servants have plenty of food. But I am here, almost dying with hunger. I will leave and return to my father. I'll say to him: Father, I have sinned against God and against you. I am not good enough to be called your son. But let me be like one of your servants." So the son left and went to his father.

'While the son was still a long way off, his father saw him coming. He felt sorry for his son. So the father ran to him, and hugged and kissed him. The son said, "Father, I have sinned against God and against you. I am not good enough to be called your son." But the father said to his servants, "Hurry! Bring the best clothes and put them on him. Also, put a ring on his finger and sandals on his feet. And get our fat calf and kill it. Then we can have a feast and celebrate! My son was dead, but now he is alive again! He was lost, but now he is found!" So they began to celebrate.

Pick three words

-

-

-

What did you learn about Jesus?

Izzy and Me

Chapter 9 – Saturday

Do you have traditions? At home? At school?

Izzy	Me
With aprons with Gran, how we always hug each other when we put them on.	

How could you 'not go on being angry all day' (Ephesians 4:26)?

Izzy	Me
Say sorry to people. Tell Jesus when I am angry.	

Write down a good thing in your life. Might it be a bester/blessing from Jesus?

Izzy	Me
Scraping out lots of cake mixture in the bowl was really good! I never thought of it as a bester, but yes, I think it is.	

Word Book

Izzy	Me
Brilliant!!!	

Here's the story you read in Chapter 9. It's in the Bible:

John 2:1–11

Two days later there was a wedding in the town of Cana in Galilee. Jesus' mother was there. Jesus and his followers were also invited to the wedding. When all the wine was gone, Jesus' mother said to him, 'They have no more wine.'

Jesus answered, 'Dear woman, why come to me? My time has not yet come.'

His mother said to the servants, 'Do whatever he tells you to do.'

In that place there were six stone water jars. The Jews used jars like these in their washing ceremony. Each jar held about 20 or 30 gallons.

Jesus said to the servants, 'Fill the jars with water.' So they filled the jars to the top.

Then he said to them, 'Now take some out and give it to the master of the feast.'

So the servants took the water to the master. When he tasted it, the water had become wine. He did not know where the wine came from. But the servants who brought the water knew. The master of the wedding called the bridegroom and said to him, 'People always serve the best wine first. Later, after the guests have been drinking a lot, they serve the cheaper wine. But you have saved the best wine till now.'

So in Cana of Galilee, Jesus did his first miracle. There he showed his glory, and his followers believed in him.

Pick three words

-

-

-

What did you learn about Jesus?

Izzy and Me

Chapter 10 – Sunday/Epilogue

Have you ever been nervous?

Izzy	Me
Yes! About going to church!	

Have you ever been to church?

Izzy	Me
Only once, but I want to go again.	

What are you thankful for today?

Izzy	Me
My Bible :-)	

Izzy and Me

These are the verses Izzy read:

Before the world began, there was the Word. The Word was with God, and the Word was God. He was with God in the beginning. All things were made through him. Nothing was made without him. In him there was life. That life was light for the people of the world. The Light shines in the darkness. And the darkness has not overpowered the Light.

John 1:1–5

Which words would you choose? The same as Izzy, or different?

Word Book

Izzy	Me
Word	
God	
Light	

Nothing can separate us from the love God has for us.

Romans 8:38

Prayer

Jesus,

Thank you that you want to be my friend.

Izzy was right. It's nice to have a friend with me all the time.

Right now, I'm looking forward to

………………………………..

I'm worried about …………………………………………

My words today are …………. …………. …………

I'm glad you listen to me and help me.

I like being friends with you.

Amen.

Do you want to read more of the Bible?

Then get your copy of *The International Children's Bible!*

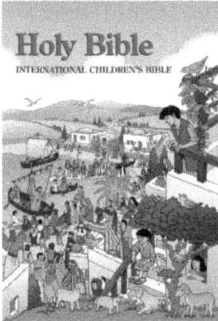

| HB: 9780850099010 | HB: 9781860244315 | PB: 9781788931465 |

The *International Children's Bible* is not an adult Bible especially packaged for children. It has specifically been translated directly from the Hebrew and Greek texts into English so that it can be read and understood by children between the ages of 6 and 12.

The *ICB* is a full text Bible that every child will be delighted to own. With guidance, daily Bible reading can easily become a pleasurable habit that will last a lifetime.

Features of the full *ICB* include:
• Large, easy to read type in two columns
• Simple footnotes explain names, customs and phrases
• 32 full colour illustrations with multicultural images
• A dictionary helps explains difficult words and phrases
• Presentation page
• Colour maps
• Ribbon marker

With simpler language and extra notes and helps, the *ICB* is the perfect Bible for a child who is ready to move on from a picture Bible to a full text Bible.

Loved reading *Izzy's Unexpected Week?*

Why not try *My Diary* and discover
more about Emily's own story?

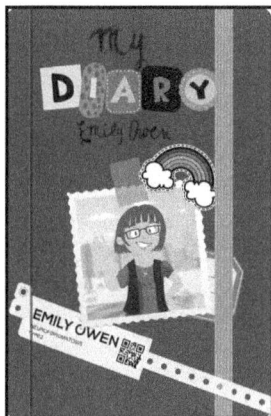

978-1-78893-166-3

Emily Owen was an energetic teenager who loved music – and life.
But dreams of becoming a teacher, enjoying music and sport all
crashed as she was given the shocking news that she had tumours in
her brain that would lead to deafness.

Emily's life would be completely different from the one she had
planned. But she had a choice. Could she let go of the life she had
hoped to live – and live a life wholly focused on God?

Read on for a sneak peak of *My Diary!*

Nightmare!

Nightmare! Mum wants me to keep a diary and write down things that happen in my life. What a silly idea – I don't really have anything to write. My life's fine, but it's not exactly exciting. Interesting stuff doesn't happen to me, but I promised Mum I'd try, so I will. Here goes . . .

I feel so stupid

My chin hurts. It's so boring, sitting here on blue plastic chairs in the hospital waiting room. Yes, I did say hospital, and all because I fell off the trampoline in gymnastics, in front of everyone, and I landed on my chin. There was blood everywhere, all over the floor of the gym and dripping onto my leotard, so the teacher sent me to hospital. What's worse than being at the hospital? Being at the hospital in a leotard. With a plaster on my chin. What a great look – not.

I need to see a doctor and get my chin sewn up. Here we go again . . .

But I suppose I should start at the beginning and explain who I am. I'm only telling you, though.

It's alright if you read my diary, but I don't want anyone else to see it, OK?

This is me

I am Emily. Thirteen years old. Tall, skinny, knobbly knees. I got called 'Mummy Longlegs' at junior school, which I hated but pretended I didn't mind. I've got three little sisters, who are fine – most of the time. Sometimes they really wind me up, though! They're called Sophie, Kirsty and Pollyanna.

I like running, and hockey, and any sport, really, except football. And except gymnastics now.

I'm good at English but rubbish at maths. I like music; I play the flute and the piano. I go to church (I used to get bullied for that). My family don't have a TV. I don't mind that – I prefer reading books anyway – but people think it's weird. I used to get bullied for that as well. People can be really mean.

I have some nice friends. I like my life, except for the bullies, and except when it means I have to be in hospital in the Accident and Emergency department (A&E), like now. I hope they call my name to see the doctor soon. I just want to get out of here.

Three stitches

I've got three stitches on my chin. They're called butterfly stitches. I have no idea why they're called that; butterflies are nice, aren't they, but these stitches aren't. They itch, not to mention looking a bit silly. White plasters on my chin. I didn't like the butterfly name the first time, either . . . which reminds me: I need to tell you why I said 'Here we go again . . .'.

When I was 11, I was skipping, trying to do 100 skips as fast as I could. I got to number 67, and then . . . Well, OK, it might not have been exactly 67, but it was about that. Anyway, the skipping rope tangled in my feet, and I fell over and landed on my chin. Can you guess what's coming? Blood, hospital, blue plastic chairs, doctor, butterfly stitches. The only difference was that it was a trampoline not a skipping rope that did it today. Oh, and the skipping rope time I was not wearing a leotard.

Egg sandwiches

Stitches on my chin and bruises, but do I get a day off school? No way. My mum would probably need me to have my arm chopped off before she'd think about letting me have a day off. She gave me egg sandwiches for my lunch today, though, so I think she does feel a bit sorry for me!

I walk to school with some of my friends. One sets off, then calls for another on the way, and so it goes on. I'm the third one to be called for, and by the time we get to school there are four of us.

Recently, the others have been laughing and saying I walk further than them, even though I live second nearest to school. I laugh about it, too, and they're right! The thing is, I can't seem to walk in a straight line. When I walk with them, they walk straight, but I wobble from side to side. I can't remember when that started, but it's become so normal now, it doesn't really bother me. Do you think it's OK not to be able to walk straight?

It would bother me if I couldn't run, but when I run I don't wobble. Weird, isn't it?!

Good thing, really, because I run in lots of races. I don't normally win, but I often come second or third. I love running.

※

Duets

The doctor took the stitches off and said my chin is healing up well. I still feel stupid about the whole thing – well, wouldn't you feel a bit stupid?! – but now at least I won't be reminded about it every time I look in a mirror.

Or every time I play my flute. Have you ever tried playing a flute with bruises on your chin? It really hurts, but it's still better than not playing. Music is my world. I'm practising duets with my sister at the moment. Duet means where two people play music together. Sophie plays clarinet, and I play flute. Duets don't really work if one person doesn't play, and anyway, I love making music. At least my chin didn't make it harder to play the piano, though now I think of it, I should have used it as an excuse! When I have my piano lesson, my teacher always seems to know I haven't practised. I love playing the piano, but I don't like practising the same old exercises again and again, so I don't, but she always seems to know! I should have thought to say I couldn't practise because of my chin. I don't think she'd have believed me. Ha ha!

But I really like my teacher; she's great. And at the end of the lesson, she always stays a bit longer to play duets with me.

No sand in my shoes!

Soon it'll be time for me to run the 800m race for my school. That means twice round the track. I'm glad I was picked for 800m, it's my best distance. I'm doing stretches now, to warm up ready for the race. When I turn my head to loosen up my neck muscles, I can see the sandpit. I'm glad I don't have to do the long jump and land in the sand and get sand in my shoes. I hate getting sand in my shoes.

I saw you jump

I have got sand in my shoes now. Don't laugh! The person who should have done the long jump was ill, and when the teacher asked me to jump instead, there was no question I'd do it. This is sport!

What's amazing is that I came in second, even though I've hardly ever tried the long jump. I still couldn't wait to get the sand out of my shoes, though! As I walked away from the sandpit with my dad, who always watches me doing sport, a man came up to us. He was wearing a tracksuit, and he looked really sporty. He said, 'Hi, I saw you jump. You're good. I want you to join my athletics club.' I thought he was joking, or maybe talking to someone behind me, but when I turned round, there was no one there. He *was* talking to me. I looked at Dad. Then I looked back at the man, and I asked him what it would involve. He said, 'Coming every Sunday and training with the club.'

God or sport?

Oh. You know I said before that I go to church? I go on Sundays. I've never not wanted to go. Well, nearly never. There was one time, when I was maybe 11, when I decided I wasn't going to church any more. People at school didn't go, so why should I? I knew it wouldn't go down well with my parents, but I was old enough to make my own decisions. I told Mum firmly one Sunday morning that I was not going to church with the rest of them, and I would just stay at

home. Well, I thought I said it firmly, but Mum didn't! She said, 'Of course you're coming with us, get in the car.' And that was that, I got in the car. I sat there, feeling really mad that I had to be there, and trying to think how I could make sure everyone in the car knew. In the end, I announced, in my crossest voice, 'Just so you know, my body is here, but I'm not.' Then I turned away from them all and stared out of the window. That'll show them, I thought. Then I heard Mum laughing! Can you believe it? She thought I'd said something funny. Anyway, in the end, I calmed down, remembered I like church, and I love God, and that was the end of my 'rebellion'. Church was, and still is, a big part of my life.

So there I am, standing with sand in my shoes, and there's a man in a tracksuit asking me to join his club. It felt like I was being asked to choose between God and sport.

Both things I love. But it didn't take me long to choose. I love God more than anything, even sport. So I said no to the athletics club.

I also decided to get baptized, to show that God comes first in my life, and I want to follow him. Here's a top tip: if you get baptized by full immersion like I did, do not wear a skirt. I wore a skirt and as I went down into the water, my skirt floated to the top!

Broken glass

I said no to long jump, but I didn't say no to running. Every Saturday in winter, my friend Katie calls for me, and we go and race for our school. We love cross-country running! Except today didn't work out as planned.

Katie rang the doorbell, which was fine. I heard it and went to answer it, which was fine. What wasn't fine was the thing that happened next. There is a mat on the floor near the door; my mum says it's to protect the carpet, but I don't know why the carpet needs protecting.

Today, I tripped on the mat, put out my hand to stop me falling, and my hand reached the door. The door has lots of glass in it, and you can probably guess what happened next! Imagine it from Katie's point of view:

She rings the bell, and waits for the door to open. Instead of the door opening, she sees a hand – my hand – break through the glass and move towards her. Oh, and my hand was dripping blood.

It was like something out of a horror movie. No wonder Katie screamed and ran home! It's a good thing she only lives across the road.

I think my mum heard her scream. Or maybe I screamed, too; I don't know. Anyway, Mum came, saw what had happened, ran to the kitchen, grabbed a towel and came and wrapped it round my wrist (most of the blood was coming from my wrist). Then Mum wrapped her hands tightly round the towel and held my arm up as high as she could. I found out later that helps slow the bleeding down, but at the time all I could think about was that it hurt.

Mum yelled for Dad to come, sent my sisters over to Katie's house and shoved me into the car – still squeezing my wrist and holding my arm in the air – and Dad drove us to the hospital as fast as he could.

So, right now, I'm sitting on a blue plastic chair. Again! No prizes for guessing where I am. My wrist and hand have a bandage now, not a towel. At least it's my left hand, so I can still write this and tell you what's happening. A doctor put the bandage on, but now I need to see another doctor. When the first one looked at my wrist, I looked at it too, and it does look bad; I can see why Katie screamed. There's this big cut on the side, just below my hand. You can see right in, right down to the tendon. The tendon is white, and I thought it was bone, but the doctor told me it's a tendon. Then he got some tweezers and pulled at the tendon. When he pulled it, my little finger moved. I was nearly sick! It's really weird seeing my finger move when I didn't move it. Eugh.

Stay

I'm home now. So relieved. They nearly didn't let me come home! When I saw the second doctor, he looked at my wrist and then said I'd need to stay in hospital tonight and have an operation tomorrow. Stay in hospital? I can't think of anything worse. Don't tell anyone, but I started to cry. I'm a bit embarrassed about that, but I was so scared. The doctor felt sorry for me and had another look at my wrist, then said he'd sew it up right away, and I could go home. He's the best doctor ever. He sewed the cut up, then put a massive bandage on, and I came home.

The Cartographer's Presence

An adventure in Aratae'Tor

Stephen Reed

Arcos is a young artist who travels to the mountainous land of Aratae'Tor for the annual Festival to honour the Cartographer who mapped out the world. But after an earthquake left his mother unable to walk, he secretly questions whether the Cartographer really loves him and his family.

Arcos is encouraged to look for the Misaro'Deio, the Cartographer's Servant, who the old prophecies say is coming soon and will turn people's hearts back to the Cartographer. He then meets Ishua who seems to know everything about him.

Could this be the Misaro'Deio? Will he change Arcos's mind about the Cartographer? And will his life ever be the same again?

978-1-78893-294-3

Hang out with the disciples and find out
what Jesus' story is all about!

PB: 9781788930291

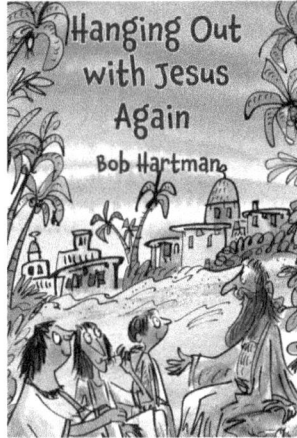

PB: 9781788931199

Big Bart, Tommo and me, Pip. Three guys on a three-year adventure, hanging out with Jesus, finding out what he's up to. Not exactly the best known of the twelve disciples, but we're on the edge of the action – out of the limelight, where there is plenty of partying, messing about and time to make idiots of ourselves.

We're best mates. And Jesus' mates, too. Every day with Jesus is so special, I've written the stories down; stories you'll find in the Bible if you take a look. Well, sort of, because everything is just a little bit different when you're hanging out with us.

Authentic

We trust you enjoyed reading this book from Authentic. If you want to be informed of any new titles from this author and other releases you can sign up to the Authentic newsletter by scanning below:

Online:
authenticmedia.co.uk

Follow us: